Book I An Honorless Moon

Mending the Promise

Emir Keithford

Chapter 1

Long ago, there was only a forever-expanding white void of nothingness. However, in that void a being floated endlessly called the Existence. He was a perfect being of indescribable appearance. It was believed he didn't have a source. He just existed and always had. The Existence did nothing but think. Until one fateful day. *It was time for a change,* he thought to himself. This mere thought brimmed with a mighty power. "I have a plan," he said to himself. More and more thoughts of what-could-be formed within his mind. The thoughts culminated into a massive explosion! It was so powerful it caused a tear in the fabric of reality. Darkness slowly moved over the whiteness of the void. Stars glowed in the darkness. The Existence had done it: The Universe was born.

He entered the Universe. The first thing the Existence did was create a top of the Universe. He called it "Paradise." The Existence claimed Paradise as his home. However, the Universe began to fall endlessly due the presence of Paradise. To resolve this, The Existence willed into existence a bottom to the Universe and named it "Hell." The Existence stopped there for the day and looked upon his work. Paradise was a pure white space that stretched on top of the Universe endlessly. It was filled with clouds, buildings of intricate design, and ethereal beings called angels. In a likewise manner, Hell stretched across the bottom endlessly. It was filled with rough rocky structures and sulfur smoke. Then the Existence realized something. He was alone. The only being of his kind. The Existence grew sick of it.

With a single thought, he envisioned seven humanoid figures with an otherworldly beauty. Seven eggs, no larger than his fists, appeared and floated around him. Not long after, the eggs hatched. The Existence's first children were born. They were called the Firstborn. The small children smiled at their father. He held them in his arms and joyously laughed. He had done it. He had a family.

The Existence debated on what names and purposes to give them. The first The Existence named was a young boy, who he named Davith.[1] He had given his son the Responsibility of Trust. The Existence wanted his children to always be able to rely on him. Davith was the peacemaker amongst the Firstborn. He was quick with his tongue and always wanted to be right. Everything Davith did (he proclaimed) was to be as much like his father as he could.

---

[1] Dah-vith

The next child he named was Nuana,[2] a daughter. She was given the Responsibility of Innocence. The Existence wanted his children to never know about evil. Nuana was a bit naïve, but never a fool. She often carried a harp and sang beautiful songs. Her graceful voice would fill the halls of Paradise with bliss and calm.

The next was Dathys,[3] another daughter. He had given her the Responsibility of Order. The Existence always wanted there to be order and unity amongst his children. As a result, Dathys always wanted everything to be perfect. She would often get upset if things were not to her standards. While Dathys did come off as demanding at times, she ultimately just wanted perfection to minimize disputes between her siblings.

The next was another boy. The Existence named him Edis.[4] Edis was given the Responsibility of Health. He insured that his siblings were always of sound mind and body. He often asked the Existence about how to mend afflictions of the mind and body. He was studious, observant, and always willing to help to his siblings.

Next was Aldin.[5] He was given the Responsibility of Justice. His job was to absolve and mediate disputes Davith couldn't handle. He often asked his Father of what he considered moral and immoral. He made it his mission to carry out justice. Aldin

---

[2] New-ahn-a

[3] Dah-this

[4] Ehd-is

[5] All-din

carried a scale that could weigh the details of the opposing parties' truths.

The next child was a boy. The Existence named him Chorasil.[6] The Existence had given him the responsibility of Luck and Fortune. He was given this purpose to bring luck and good deeds to his other siblings. And of course, himself. The Existence reminded him have to remind him of the dangers of greed and how he must determine how one's fortune could affect another's fortune. His responsibility was not perfect, but his actions were fair and admirable.

The last of the Firstborn was given the name of Theosorh,[7] and he was given the Responsibility of Logic. He was provided this to allow his siblings to be wise in their choices and dealings with each other. His mind was often factual and devoid of emotions. Due to his apathetic nature, it was difficult for him to be around his other siblings. He would often cling to the Existence and would talk of the Universe and its schematics.

As time went on, The Existence's children came of age; they were no longer the little boys and girls he knew—they became men and women who could stand on their own. But the Existence noticed a change in them . . . and it was disturbing. He could see the greed in their hearts, but in his own foolishness, he chose to ignore the sounds.

One day, Davith approached The Existence and said unto him, "Father, I must speak to you."

---

[6] Chore-a-sill

[7] Theo-sore

"Yes, my son?" he said.

"My siblings and I have grown up and we have noticed how you treat the universe. And we don't like the way it is being created."

His eyes widened with shock and he asked, "What is it you do not like, my son?"

"This universe revolves only around you yet makes no mention of us. Your angels greatly admire you and treat us merely as miniscule things. We do not like it," replied Davith.

"And what would you propose, my son?" asked the Existence.

"We wish to create the Universe in our own image," said Davith.

"Absolutely not! Where have these ideas come from?" responded The Existence.

"They simply are, old man," said Davith.

"Leave my sight, Son. We will discuss this later," said The Existence.

Davith bowed his head and then said, "Very well."

I fear for the future, The Existence thought.

Chapter 2

Davith stormed the halls of Paradise. He grumbled and muttered to himself. He felt a welling sense of hurt and pride. He thought to himself, *All these years and he still sees us as feeble children. This cannot stand.* He approached his fellow siblings and gathered them to a secluded location. The first that he called to his side was his sister Nuana.

"Why have you gathered us, Brother? Father's word is law. It would not be just to disobey him," said Aldin, the first to chime in.

"Aldin, silence. Can you not think for yourself? Who is to say that his word MUST be the law? Why does Father cast these 'Responsibilities' upon us?! Is he too lazy to perform them himself?" spouted Davith.

Nuana approached Davith and caressed his cheek, "My love, are you sure it is wise for us to disobey our Father? He did create us after all. He sees us as family just as much as we see each other."

"Yet you fraternize with each other as lovers. How vile," rebuked Dathys. Davith gently lowered his lover's hand and replied, "We do not have to justify our love to you all, but you must agree with me that there must be a change, right?" The whole room is silent for a moment before Chorasil chimed in, "What is your plan, Brother?"

And so, the night went on as Davith explained his plan to the others: They would assassinate their own Father using blades crafted from the finest cosmic metal. They crafted daggers from the Void. They figured by using what The Existence used to create them and the Universe would be strong enough to slay him as well. They just had to get him away from his horde of angels. The annoying little autonomous birds. Their scheming went relatively unnoticed. Even by Jamaerah, considered the wittiest and fairest of all angels. He was such an obedient bird.

However, a lesser angel had overheard the plan of the Firstborn and immediately flew over to The Existence. "My Lord! I have urgent news!" said the little angel. His wings collapsed on the ground. He struggled to catch his breath.

"What is it, Zabkiel?" asked the Existence. He took the small being into his hand.

After he caught his breath, Zabkiel responded, "It concerns your children. I overheard them talking. They intend to slaughter you, My Lord!"

"Slaughter? Nonsense. My children would do nothing of the sort," said the Existence with a serious tone in his voice.

Zabkiel pleaded, "But—"

"No buts. I shall confront my children myself on this. Away with you," said the Existence. He gently let the angel take to flight from his hand. Zabkiel gave the Existence a look of concern but did as he was told.

The following day, the Existence approached the Firstborn. They were casually laying down in the garden of Paradise. Davith smiled and said, "Good morning, Father! How are you?"

"I am well, Davith, but there is an urgent matter I must discuss with you all." The Firstborn's eyes lit up and looked at their Father. "One of my angels overheard something that you were all discussing," stated the Existence bluntly. He chuckled for moment and then said, "They said you intend to kill me for denying your request at building the Universe to your own whims."

The Firstborn looked at each other for a moment. They began to laugh heartily as Davith replied, "Murder you? Nonsense! We'd never do anything of the sort!"

"Very well . . ." said the Existence. He then walked out of the Garden.

That night, the Firstborn enacted their attack on their Father. Nuana and Davith carried a blade of the Void. The blades were shiny, the edges appeared as light. Nuana was giggling, but Davith shushed her to silence. The Existence was asleep in his chambers. He was snoring very loudly. The two surrounded his bed. They looked upon him with obsession and aggression in their eyes. Davith was the first to attack! He unsheathed his dagger and gave a powerful stab. The knife went right through their Father's heart. A glowing rift appeared before slowly closing back up. The Existence's eyes immediately opened to see his precious Davith and Nuana over him, daggers in their hands. With a single will of thought, he pushed them both back. He tearfully asked, "My children . . . what has become of you?!" The Firstborn ran out of their Father's chamber.

The Existence knew that there was no place for them to go. He simply let them run and he contemplated. He agonized on how to process the fact that his own children tried to kill him. They should have known it wouldn't work, yet they still tried. He felt that there could have been a way that his children and he could have worked this out. But now the fact was that this injustice could not stand. "Vigil, summon the troops," said The Existence, unemotional and almost robotic.

With a sounding of Vigil's war horn, legions of angels began to fly in the skies of Paradise. The Firstborn tried to hide, but they could not hide from the retribution of their Father. The Firstborn slaughtered several angels but they were vastly outnumbered. They were captured alive. The Firstborn were chained and brought in front of their Father's throne. The Existence was armed with a mystical blade of gold.

The Existence looked upon them and asked, "Have you no words for your treachery? Your misdeeds?" Davith simply stared and looked at him. He then took a brief look at Nuana. The Existence shook his head in disappointment.

"So, what will you do with us, Father? Kill us to preserve your precious Universe?" asked Davith.

The Existence looked at the sword and Vigil, the angel, stepped up. Vigil said, "My Lord. You should not have to carry this burden. Allow me to—"

The Existence lifted a hand to him and said, "No. This is my responsibility. Speaking of which, I strip you all of your Responsibilities." The influence of the Responsibilities left the Firstborn.

The Existence contemplated what to do. He could not bring himself to sever the heads of his children. And after some consideration, he said unto them, "You no longer are allowed here. I strip away your rights to exist in this domain. You are forbidden."

"Oh Father! You cannot mean that!" said Chorasil.

"No, please. Forgive us, Father!" implored Edis. The Firstborn clamored and begged for this fate not to befall them . . . all except Davith, who had a maddened and uproarious stare upon their Father. And in an instant, they floated in nothingness. They were within the Void, stripped of all except their names.

They began to weep and contemplated their new lives within the Void. But eventually the weeping stopped for them. However, The Existence continued to weep over the punishment he had dealt to his Firstborn. The Firstborn became known as the Forbidden Ones. Eventually, it became an unspoken rule to not speak of them in The Existence's presence. The Forbidden cast aside their old names and began to adopt their own Motives. These Motives were the opposite of what they once were. Davith became Hti'vad,[8] Motivator of Betrayal. Nuana became

---

[8] Huh-ti-vad

Nuipex,[9] Hti'vad's wife as well as Motivator of Corruption. Dathys became Vh'ela,[10] Motivator of Chaos. Edis adopted the name of Scar-li-homun,[11] Motivator of Disease. Aldin became V'alko,[12] Motivator of Revenge. Theosorh became Ithygriss,[13] Motivator of Insanity. And Chorasil became Aishidd'k,[14] Motivator of Misfortune.

---

[9] New-pecs

[10] Vuh-hella

[11] Scar-lee-ho-mun

[12] Vall-co

[13] Ith-thee-grus

[14] Uh-shed-kuh

Chapter 3

That night, The Existence lay in bed. His house was devoid of the laughter of his children. Just like the Void—solitude even with his angelic servants. *What have I done? I should go get them. We should talk . . . no, what they did was inexcusable. Perhaps some time in the Void will do them and me some good,* he thought to himself. The Existence wept himself to sleep.

He awakened and thought to himself, *What a horrible nightmare. I hope to never have another like it.*

Vigil asked, "My Lord, are you all right?"

"Me? Of course! I just had a rough nightmare that I sent my own children into the Void," responded The Existence.

Vigil paused for a moment. "Um, forgive me, Lord, but . . . you did do that."

"Of course not! Don't be silly; that would make me the worst Father in existence if I did something like that!" said The Existence.

Vigil put a hand on The Existence's shoulder. "My Lord . . . I cannot imagine how hard this is for you. But you must face facts. Your children grew up and wanted to do harm to the Universe, and tried to kill you to achieve that. The other angels and I are here for you. One does not simply 'bounce back' from such a trauma. This wound will take time to heal." Vigil flew away.

The Existence walked though Paradise. *It should have been me cast out. I should have just left this Universe and given it to them. This is my fault. I expected too much out of them. Those Responsibilities must have been too much. They must have been so stressed. I'm a horrible Father.* The Existence sat down on a bench and waved to his angels. The Void was in plain view. His children appeared as simply small dots in the distance. He immediately recoiled from the thought he had. "No, no. They need time still. I should let them figure it out. Maybe . . . I need to figure things out as well? I just want my family back," said The Existence to himself.

The Existence constructed more planets in the Universe. He willed a stone and molded it before tossing it into the abyss. "No, no, no. This is all wrong!" He threw a ball of fire at the cluster of planets he just made. They all exploded. The Existence groaned and pinched his eyebrows. He said to himself, "None of this matters. Why do I bother? Damn it all!" He slammed his fist into a galaxy and it shattered into nothingness. The Existence sighed once more.

The next day, the Lord lay in bed once more. Angels constantly flocked to him. They would often ask, "Are you all right, my Lord?" "Is there anything we can do for you?" "We are here for you."

To which The Existence would reply: "I will be okay." "No thank you." "Thank you."

Most angels in the early days were robotic and emotionless. No better than automatons. The only angels who the Existence had given sentience were his archangels, notably Vigil and Jamaerah. Jamaerah waited at The Existence's bedside and after several hours passed, Jamaerah said, "It is not your fault that your children rebelled. They were fools not to realize that they would never be able to defeat you. Why feel such remorse for them?"

"It is not that simple, Jamaerah. They were my children," responded The Existence.

"Oh? Simply because you created them? You created us as well; are we not considered your children as well?" retorted Jamaerah.

"It's complicated. I literally raised them from small timid children until they were adults. You were spawned as adults, fully capable of thought," said the Existence. "Not to start out.

Most of us are autonomous beings that follow your will. Between me, Vigil, and the other archangels, it is boring," said Jamaerah.

"What would you suggest?" asked the Existence.

"Why not give the other angels as much reason as Vigil and I possess? Perhaps it would liven up Paradise" said Jamaerah.

"I will think on it, Jamaerah. Leave me for now, please. I have things to think upon," said the Existence. Jamaerah nodded and left The Existence's chamber.

The Existence headed into the Void via a projection. Davith and the others' once fair and beautiful forms had changed, being now without reason or logical shape—a mass of tendrils, vague humanoid shapes, and other oddities. Davith simply looked at his Father. His eyes were bloodshot, a murderous glare in them. He asked, "What do you want?"

"I came to talk," replied the Existence.

"Then speak," said Davith from his throne built from nothing. His sister, now his Queen, sat upon his lap.

The Existence said, "I would . . . like to discuss what happened."

"All these years . . . and you have decided you cannot bear it anymore?" replied Davith.

"Years? But it has been merely months, my child," said The Existence.

"In the Void, time moves differently. Seconds to the Universe are like minutes here and vice versa. It has been years . . . and now you come because you feel bad? Pathetic old man," said Davith.

The Existence said, "But my son . . ."

"I AM NO LONGER YOUR SON! You are nothing to us. Leave us or fight," said Davith as other eyes affixed on The Existence's projection.

The Existence nodded and left. The Existence sobbed within his chamber.

A small tear ran down Davith's face, his heart still pained for his mistakes. He kissed Nuana.

Jamaerah walked in and said, "So you finally decided to do it. How did they look?"

"Awful. I barely recognized them," said The Existence.

"I'm sorry," said Jamaerah.

"Thank you," said The Existence.

"I apologize for snooping on you. I was growing concerned when you kicked me out so suddenly," said Jamaerah. He sat next to The Existence.

"That is all right...so you mentioned something about allowing angels to be freer?" asked The Existence

"Indeed," said Jamaerah.

"I have an idea for that," said The Existence.

And after much back and forth dialogue with Jamaerah and Vigil, The Existence established what he called Natures. The Nature of Instinct and the Nature of Free Will. The Nature of Instinct instilled those who possessed it rudimentary knowledge of themselves to survive. The Nature of Free Will allowed beings to Choose and those decisions impacted their Fate. He instilled the angels with each property and Jamaerah smiled. Jamaerah had never smiled since he was created.

Jamaerah was in the garden with several angels. He talked and played with them. "Videl, what do you think of our Lord, the Existence?" asked Jamaerah.

"He is our creator and a wonder leader, of course!" said Videl.

"Are you sure of that?" said Jamaerah.

"What do you mean, Jamaerah?" asked Uriel.

"Just suggesting that The Existence isn't exactly as 'pious' and 'great' as you all think. I hear that he had 'known' a few other angels. 'Extra' training for his soldiers. And he snatched food from one of the younger angels, the bastard," said Jamaerah. The angels gasped and Jamaerah sowed the first seeds of deception.

Chapter 4

Eventually, Jamaerah built his spheres of influence amongst his angelic brethren. The majority stayed on the Lord's side, but the minority that clung to Jamaerah's side geared up for war. Jamaerah commissioned a set of specially made chains, crafted from the feathers of Metatron, The Existence's lesser manifestation. He had them plucked from Metatron while he befriended The Existence.

The Existence was aware of Jamaerah's actions. A fraction of his angels intended to disobey him. With a simple Will of Thought, he crafted himself armor of shimmering celestial gold as well as a spear that shone brighter than several suns. He sat at his throne and waited for Jamaerah. "He seeks to rule this throne, but I should rather fade into nothingness than let it fall into his treacherous hands," said The Existence.

"Such trying times we live in. I remember a time when Jamaerah was another loyal servant of yours," said Vigil.

As time continues, people change. I now see the dangers of these Natures . . . how easy they can be corrupted. I must be careful about the next phase of my Plan, thought The Existence. The gate of Paradise was broken in.

The Jamaerah-allied angels' armor was obsidian black. Their eyes glowed with an intense red. The Existence waved his hand and his silver-armored angels charged against Jamaerah's forces. The Lord threw fireballs at some of the angels. He summoned Metatron, who pummeled through the horde of rebellious angels. Jamaerah descended, his six wings steadily losing feathers. "If you give up now, I may show you mercy," said Metatron.

"Why does your puppet speak to me but not yourself, Creator? Afraid to lose?" said Jamaerah as he slit the throat of an angel.

"I'm not afraid to lose; I'm afraid of the things I will do to you once your forces are defeated," said the Existence.

Jamaerah spat in reply and bound Metatron with chains. The manifestation fell to the ground. Jamaerah's angels stabbed his limbs. The Existence broke his link to Metatron.

The Existence stabbed the spear into the ground. The shockwave blew the angels back. The Existence still did not move from his throne. Jamaerah charged at The Existence, but he was stopped by a juggernaut of force. Jamaerah summoned his angels to him and they charged up a massive blackened beam of energy, but the field did not budge. "Coward! Fight me yourself!" yelled Jamaerah.

"Very well," said The Existence. He snapped his fingers, bringing the battle to a halt. The angels were suspended in air. Time had been frozen. The Existence shut down his field and stood up from his throne. The Existence walked down the great steps and Jamaerah landed on the ground, chain and sword in hand.

They circled each other, eyeing one another. The Existence struck first, lunging with his spear. Jamaerah dodged the lunge and tried to stab The Existence in the eye with his blade. The Existence easily caught the sword and snapped it in half. Jamaerah tossed the chain around the Existence's arm. The burning sensation of the chain seeped into The Existence's being and Jamaerah pulled the Lord forward. He knocked his helmet off. The Existence grabbed Jamaerah by the throat and slammed him into the ground, cracking the foundation of Paradise, sending them falling into the Universe. The Existence grunted as he tried to pull the chain off his arm. Jamaerah dragged him down and they wrestled.

The Existence put Jamaerah in a full nelson and Jamaerah wrapped the chain around The Existence's leg. The Existence grunted as he felt the burning sensation on his leg. "Give it up. You are an arrogant, vapid ruler who only thinks of himself!" said Jamaerah.

"Fool, I care for all of my creations—including you! Give up now and there is still forgiveness for you!" yelled the Existence.

"NEVER! DIE!" yelled Jamaerah.

He threw Jamaerah into a planet, splitting the massive sphere in two. The Existence slammed into him harder, completely destroying the planet. "I shall tear those wings that I blessed you out of your back!" yelled The Existence as he held the malicious angel by the wings. He ripped out one pair of wings from the angel.

Jamaerah screamed and blood spewed from his back. In a shaky voice, Jamaerah said, "No wonder your children hate you."

The Existence's eyes glowed. He ripped off the bound limbs and regenerated new ones, now free of the chains. "You will regret saying that," said The Existence as he encased Jamaerah in chains. He lifted him up back into Paradise and the foundation was quickly restored.

He lined up all the angels at his throne. They had been bound in a similar way, awaiting their fate. Vigil stood Jamaerah up. The Existence willed a sword into his hand and sliced off the rest of Jamaerah's wings. "You are no longer The Light Bringer. I will punish you for your treachery. Of those of you who took part in this betrayal, you will be punished as severely as your Leader. I gave you Free Will and you did this? I cast you to live in the Flooring, otherwise known as Hell. You are no longer angels . . . you are demons. And you, 'O Leader,' I curse you. I curse you to be all that there is negative in the world: dread, sorrow, hate, evil . . . all these are now forever bonded to you. You are no longer Jamaerah; I shall call you the Adversary." The Existence cast the Adversary and his ilk into Hell, where they all screamed and begged . . . as they plummeted down.

Chapter 5

The Existence grew lonely once again and created more children from various elements of the Universe. They were a race of beings called the Primordial Titans. The Titans each controlled dominion over their element.

The First was Umbra, molded from the darkness of the Universe. He was called Biggest Brother amongst his little siblings. He was the oldest amongst the Titans, and he was also the largest. To human scale, he would be about eight feet tall, but could grow much larger as he deemed fit.

Sol was crafted from the light. He was a very energetic being and one of Father's favorites. Despite the framing of light being good, he was always cruel to his younger siblings.

Stone was crafted from the rock and dirt of space debris. Very eccentric yet a master of crafting things. To an almost obsessive degree, in many ways he was more like Father than he ever realized.

Aqueon was formed from the water of a nearby space ocean. As the middle child, she grew tired of her siblings' antics and being ignored by Father. Yet she was one of the most important Titans for livings beings.

Aeolian was molded from the very breath of Father. He was so carefree, always riding the winds. He was very lackadaisical.

Fyreon was created from the flames of a collapsed star. She had a very volatile temper and always wanted to get her way. Father was the only one who could often quell her bratty rage.

Little Lun was simply willed into being . . . no element was used for him. He was called The Little One. The Runt. The Weak One. As well as many other cruel names too rude to repeat. All given to him by his younger siblings. Umbra wanted them to get along. Lun was not aware of his purpose for a very long time, yet somehow, he was the Lord's most favorite of them all.

The young Titians sang, danced, played, bonded with their Father. They gave him their love and in return, the Lord gave them more. But still . . . that fear of the Forbidden Ones loomed in the back of his mind. Lun grasped his father's hand once while he was in contemplation of this. "Don't worry, Father. I promise I will never betray you," said the young child. The Existence smiled back.

One day, the Existence gathered them together and told them to follow him into a new galaxy. It is now known as the Milky Way, which inside there was nothing but the Void. The Titans had never felt anything like it before . . . and had only seen the edges of it. The sensation to them was varied and disturbing.

The Existence took them by his massive hand and said to Umbra, "Umbra, create some darkness, please." Umbra nodded and, in an instant, the Titans floated in darkness. "Sol, create a sun and stars if you please?" Sol created stars to illuminate the darkness. He cupped his hands and released a ball of light that expanded to the Sun until The Existence said, "Enough. Thank you, Sol and Umbra." The Existence crossed his arms while they floated and said, "You're probably wondering why you are all here. That is because I am tasking you seven with your first galaxy."

"Whoa! Our own galaxy?" shouted Sol.

"And by first, I presume we will be making more than this one, right?" said Aqueon.

"Ugh. I hope not. If Father wants more galaxies, why doesn't he just get his archangels to do it for him?" whined Aeolian.

"Shut up, Aeolian. If we are making a galaxy, I'll be damned if there is no fire in it," said Fyreon. "Finally! A task worthy enough to test my craftsmanship! I thank you for this opportunity, Father," said Stone.

Umbra said nothing.

"This will be good for you all. It'll give you all a perfect field to truly test yourselves. All of you! As a matter of fact, Lun, step forward," said The Existence. The Existence put his hand on the Lun's shoulder and proclaimed, "Lun, I am placing you in charge of the construction of this galaxy!" Lun's eyes widened.

"What?! Him?! The runt?! Forget that, I'm taking charge!" said Fyreon, her body aflame and her face red. "Father, forgive me for saying this, but I highly doubt Lun could come up with a plan on how to create this galaxy. Nor a contingency plan should something go wrong.

"He knows nothing of the sciences!" cried Stone.

"Father, this is not a good idea," said Sol.

"Why does he of all of us get to be the one to lead this? You pretend I don't exist half of the time" said Aqueon.

"I'd rather have Jamaerah lead us on this than Lun, Father," said Aeolian bluntly.

Sol said, "I really don't want to question your infinite wisdom, but I really don't think this is a good idea, Father.

Umbra chimed in, "I think we should give Lun a chance, guys. He's never going to reach his potential if we keep putting him down all the time. Worst case scenario, Dad will just pick another one of us to lead instead."

"It's our first galaxy, Umbra! I'll be damned if that little runt ruins this chance for us!" yelled Fyreon.

"ENOUGH!" yelled The Existence; a shockwave made his children silent. "It has been decided that Lun WILL create this galaxy with you all and is in charge. End of discussion. Understood?" The Existence cast seven stones from his hand, and they became the basis for the planets. He said, "These are your planets. I shall be back in five days to look at your progress. Please work together and most of all, HAVE FUN!" said The Existence. He then disappeared. Lun was all alone with his siblings who hated him.

Chapter 6

Umbra came forth first, his black void-like eyes staring right at Lun. "What is the plan, Leader?" asked Umbra. Not a trace of the usual sarcasm from him. This surprised Lun. Lun then replied, "Um, I guess let's start with the first rock, I mean planet." There were some looks of skepticism amongst his siblings, but ultimately, they went to the first planet.

Sol said, "It is the closest to the Sun, so this should be mine to work on," Lun said.

"But Dad said—"

"I don't care; I'm naming this one . . . hmm . . . Solaris?" injected Sol. The other Titans disagreed with this name. Sol rolled his eyes and then responded, "Everyone's a critic. Well come on now, we must settle on a name. How about Luminus? Lighton? Come on!"

Lun suggested the name "Mercury." Sol yelled, "What?! That name has nothing to do with light!"

Aqueon smirked and said, "I actually like that name. Mercury . . . has a nice ring to it." The Titians put the name to a vote and, much to Sol's dismay, Mercury was to be its name.

"Fine. Mercury, it is," bemoaned Sol, "But it is still my planet so I shall build it!" He asked Stone to do something. With a small bit of Stone's will, the lumpy space rock was carved into a spherical shape. "And now . . . a dash of life!" said Sol. He set a wisp of light on the planet and tiny living beings had formed . . . then immediately died due the sheer heat of Mercury.

"Oh, my apologies. I did not realize you wanted life to be sustained on this planet," said Stone while he adjusted his glasses. Fyreon and Aeolian immediately burst out into laughter. Sol grumbled.

"So . . . what planet would be the best suited for life?" asked Lun.

"The Third and Fourth Planets are worthy candidates. Their distance from the Sun is ideal. The heat intensity would much less cruel to a being than it would be on Mercury. A wise question, Lun. I'm impressed," said Stone.

"Thank you, Stone," said Lun with a smile. Lun then confidently declared, "On to the next planet!"

"No fair; I want another planet," muttered Sol.

"I'll take the next one!" said Fyreon.

"Why should you get it? I think of all the people in this family, it should be me that gets it," said Aqueon.

"Not a chance, Sister. Leave this one to me. I have the perfect idea for it," said Fyreon.

Aqueon knocked the Fire Titan back. They lunged at each other but were caught by the black tendrils emanating from Umbra's cloak. "Stop it," he said, "Both of you are acting like little brats. Just for that, I'm acting as tiebreaker to this childish debate. I'm taking this planet and you are going to work TOGETHER as a FAMILY to help me make it. Sound fair, Lun? You need to be more confident and take charge." Lun simply nodded.

Fire melted down the rock to a tiny form and Aqueon summoned water to cover it. The water immediately froze. The result was a tiny speck of planet, too tiny to even technically be considered that. "I will name this planet Pluto, which in the one of the Ancient Tongues of Father means "Brat's Folly," said Umbra with a smirk.

The Titans moved on to the next planet, to which Stone had laid claim. He withdrew his hammer and chisels and carved the planet with his mighty hand into the perfect spherical shape. "Perfect!" said Stone. He held the leftover shavings of the planet's crust.

Aeolian whisked by on cosmic winds. He crashed into Stone; the wind he summoned blew the leftovers all over Stone's planet. "Oh no, I'm so sorry! Let met fix it!" exclaimed Aeolian as he willed the wind again. This created a belt of rock around the planet. "Oops, let me try again!" said Aeolian, commanding the wind once more around the planet, making the mess worse.

"Enough! Stop!" yelled Stone. He grabbed Aeolian by the shirt and said, "You've done enough! Actually . . . looking at this planet, it doesn't look half bad. I'll keep the belt on it."

"Whew, I thought you were going to kick my ass for a second there," said Aeolian as he wiped the sweat from his forehead. A massive gust of cosmic wind engulfed another planet: A gigantic ball of gas, bigger than the other planets. It was then decided Aeolian was to stay away from the rest of the planets. Stone named his planet Saturn and Aeolian named his accidental planet Jupiter.

"Lun, would it be all right if I went next? I have the perfect idea for a planet," said Aqueon. Aqueon took a planet and named it Neptune. She summoned waters which transitioned to gas and ice. She morphed the clarity of the water to a beautiful shade of blue.

"Whoa, your planet looks so pretty, Sister," said Lun.

Aqueon playfully ruffled the boy's hair before saying, "No offense. I did this not to impress you or our brother, little Lun. I did this for me. Not for Father either, it's pointless to try to do anything to impress him after all."

Lun said, "Okay then, onto the next planet—"

"I want this one, runt. Give it to me," said Fyreon. Umbra cleared his throat and waved his tendrils at his sister. Fyreon sighed, "May I please have this planet, Brother?"

"Okay!" said Lun.

"Finally! Time to test my mettle! I shall call this planet Venus! And it shall be set aflame! Behold!" said Fyreon. She drew up her

Will and the planet was molten and molded by the Fire Titan with her bare hands. "And now . . . for life!" said Fyreon as she placed a wispy ember onto the planet. The tiny life immediately died. "What!? I was sure I had made it so it would resist fire." said Fyreon.

Stone scoffed and then said, "Fool, did you not hear me before? Only the Third and Fourth Planet will be suitable for life on them. They are the only planets that will sustain life."

Fyreon sighs. "Fine, I'll just take the Four—"

"No. It's Lun's turn to make a planet," said Umbra.

"Huh?!" responded Lun.

"What?! Why him? He doesn't even have any power!" said Fyreon.

"We've all made a planet so far. Lun needs to make his own. It's only fair. Otherwise, we will have failed Father's instructions to work together. You don't want to upset Father, do you?" said Umbra. Fyreon fumed and muttered as she walked away from Biggest Brother.

"But . . . I don't know how to make a planet," said Lun.

"I'll teach you. Come here," said Umbra.

Chapter 7

Lun approached his Biggest Brother Umbra. The Darkness Titan towered over him. Umbra looked at him with those obsidian swirling eyes of his. "I'll be honest; I don't know what to do. I'm not like you guys," said Lun with his head down.

Umbra lifted up the boy's chin and said, "Always keep your head up. I'll help you." Umbra gave one of his rare smiles. The Titans approached the Fourth Planet. "First, visualize the planet. Close your eyes," instructed Umbra. Lun closed his eyes. "What do you see?' asked Umbra.

"I see a red planet. A massive plane of rivers and dunes," responded Lun.

"What is its name?" asked Umbra.

"Um . . . Mars?" replied Lun nervously.

"Don't sound so unsure—be confident in your answers. Now summon up your Will. That's your drive, the thing that moves you; feel it. Focus on it," instructed Umbra.

Lun took a breath and tried to focus on this welling energy. The boy clenched his fists and felt the force of the energy.

"Good. Now hold it in for a moment—focus on the way Mars is supposed to look. Keep breathing. Focus on the stone . . . now RELEASE!" said Umbra.

With a mighty yell, Lun released the focused energy and BOOM! Mars was born. "I-I did it!" said Lun with a smile. He looked back at his biggest brother.

Umbra smirked and said, "Not bad."

Stone inspected the planet and said, "It is adequate. Good job, Lun."

"I like the red color. I'm proud of you," said Aqueon.

"Huh, look at that. You're finally good for something, Lun," said Sol with a chuckle.

"That's a good-looking planet, Little Bro," said Aeolian.

Sol approached Lun and said to him, "So, do you think you can handle what comes next?"

"Umm, that'd be creating life, right? I don't know how to," said Lun.

Sol wrapped his arm around Lun's shoulder and said, "Don't worry. I will help you with that." Sol took Lun to the planet's surface. The other Titans watched patiently and whispered to each other. "Instruction time: So, you already made the planet, right? That's your framework. Tell me what you think goes best here," said Sol.

"Let's see . . . it's red, sandy, kind of hot, but in there's plenty of water and a decent front to accommodate that," said Lun.

"And? What does all of that wordy talk translate to?" asked Sol, arms crossed in expectation.

"Something that needs water to live? And can survive in this heat?" asked Lun.

"Okay, we're on the right track; what else? Do these creatures swim or do they walk?" asked Sol.

"Hmm—both?"

Sol nodded, "Okay. Good. Next step. Focus on the terrain. Hold out your palms. No, no. Like this," said Sol as he adjusted Lun's hands to a position like he was cupping water. "Now think of a creature. What does it look like? Can it speak? You said walking and swimming. It'll need arms and legs," said Sol.

Lun envisioned the creature: a red-skinned, box-bodied creature with its face on its torso. It was short and stubby, even compared to Lun's size. A ball of light formed in the young Titan's palms, swirling and glowing with power. "What do I do with it?" asked Lun.

"Plant it into the ground" said Sol.

Lun dug a small hole in the sands and carefully placed the ball of life into the hole and covered it with soil. The ground shook and several figures erupted from the sands. The Martians were born. One of them looked up at Lun with curious eyes. Another of them uttered a single word: "Muh." The Martian repeated the word over and over in secession until the other Martians joined in and surrounded Lun and Sol.

"What in the world is happening?" asked Lun.

"They recognize you as the one who created them. Why did you make them talk in some silly 'muh' language?" asked Sol.

"I don't know. I got nervous and that's all that came out: 'Muh.'" The Martians bowed to Lun and Sol. After that, the Martians moved around the planet.

"Regardless, not a bad start; Now let's focus on plants and the aquatic life," said Sol.

After several hours of instruction and Sol scolding Lun for his mistakes, a beautiful planet of his own design was created. Lun thought to himself, "Oh, how proud Father will be of me!" Lun lay under a tree along with a few of his siblings. They looked at the Martian skies and the little Martians running around.and watched them as they made tools for hunting and fishing—and even clothing. However, they still spoke in that bizarre "Muh" language.

Aqueon swam in the rivers Lun had created. The rivers all flowed to one giant source. Several fish and spiny-eared dorsal fish followed her. Stone inspected the terrain and kept questioning Lun about the anatomy and biology of Martian life. A tiny group of Martians with spears tried to hurt Fyreon. The group ran away after she burned a couple of them to a crisp.

"I'm proud of you, Little Brother. When Father first put you in charge, I was a bit worried that our first galaxy together was going to be a mess," said Sol.

"I believed in you the entire time," said Umbra.

"Thank you both, really. I just wish . . . I knew what I was good at," responded Lun.

"Oh?" asked Sol with an arched brow.

"You know . . . what kind of Titan I am. You're the Titan of Light. Umbra's the Titan of Darkness, Aqueon's water, Stone is earth, Aeolian's wind, Fyreon's fire, and then there's me . . . Titan of Nothing," said Lun. He frowned.

"Oh, my Child, you are certainly not the Titan of Nothing. You just haven't discovered your power yet. But you will—very sooner than you think," echoed the voice of the Existence.

Lun and his brothers got up. Sol sighed. "You need to stop putting yourself down. You made this whole planet pretty much by yourself. You will find it soon enough," said Sol.

"Okay," nodded Lun.

Aqueon walked upon the water and joined her siblings. Water effortlessly glided off her and back into the river until she was dry. "How many days have passed? We have one more planet to make," she said.

"By my count, about five or six days," responded Sol.

"Oh good. What if we all made the last one together? With Lun leading, of course," suggested Aqueon.

"I wouldn't mind that," said Stone as he held a Martian in his palm. He observed its odd features. Aeolian rode a gust over to his siblings and said, "I think we are all in agreement about that, except for one grumpy hothead." Fyreon sat by herself in the distance.

"I'll go talk to her," said Lun. He stood up and walked over to his sister.

Fyreon had a stern look on her face. "Hey," said Lun. Fyreon looked over to the little Titan for a moment before turning back. She threw a fireball at the sky. "I know you're upset about Venus; I'm sorry that happened," said Lun.

"We're the youngest of this family," said Fyreon.

"Huh?" asked Lun.

"We're the youngest. And yet, I treat you like garbage. What kind of a sister am I? I feel like I can't be happy for you," said Fyreon.

Lun stayed silent for moment and then said, "I forgive you. I want to give you a second chance. All of you actually."

Fyreon stood up and turned to him. "Why?" asked Fyreon.

"Because we're family," Lun responded. Within a flash, Fyreon hugged Lun. The Fire Titan had never hugged him or anyone except for Father before. Lun was bewildered. He thought a fallen angel had bewitched him for a moment.

The Titan Siblings walked back to the others. A booming voice echoed, "Ah, that's what I like to see: My children getting along."

"FATHER?! exclaimed the Titans in unison. Then the Existence's form appeared before the Titans. He had a huge grin on his face. The Titans tackled him in a group hug.

"What are you doing here so early, Old Man?" asked Umbra.

"Well, you were all making record time in creating this galaxy—even with Aeolian's slip up" said The Existence. Aeolian awkwardly cleared his throat and looked away. The Existence grinned and then said, "I'm proud of you all. Especially you, Lun. This planet is beautiful. And all these little Martians are adorable. Fyreon . . . your planet reminds me of you. And I love that. Aqueon, your planet is my favorite shade of blue. Stone, my son, your creativity knows no bounds. Aeolian, although your planet was made by accident, it still looks nice. A happy little accident. Umbra and Sol, my eldest children, thank you helping your siblings work together as a unit. What say you all? Let's build this final planet together!"

The Titans were all in agreement. It was now time to create the planet known as Earth. The Titans left.

Little wisps came out of the things on Mars that ceased to live. A wisp of something . . . but when Lun tried to bring up these occurrences to his siblings, they saw nothing. That was the turning point in Lun's potential. Lun felt confused. What was he seeing?

Chapter 8

The Earth started out as a little rock. The temperature of the rock was fair—not too hot, and not too cold. Stone took up his hammer and chisel. He carved the Earth into a sphere. In the Earth Titan's hand, he held the leftover shavings. He placed them into the center, creating a gigantic landmass called a continent.

Aqueon created the oceans. She flooded the planet except for the giant continent. Her power was so great, however, the water seeped into the landmass. This created rivers and streams. Aeolian filled the skies with air and clouds, creating the atmosphere. Umbra and Sol got into an argument concerning the day and night cycle. "The planet should be daylight, all of the time!" yelled Sol.

"No. It will be nightfall all the time to counteract the heat of the Sun, you glowing idiot," responded Umbra with fierce eyes.

"Boys, please stop fighting. We can come to an agreement on this," said Father.

"I've got an idea!" said Lun with a bright grin, "Why not make half the day night and half the day sunny?"

Sol and Umbra considered this for a moment. And then Sol finally said, "But wouldn't it be too cold at night for lifeforms?" Lun thought on that for a moment himself. He approached Stone and said, "Hey Stone do you have any earth leftover?" Stone nodded. Lun convinced Stone to use his last bits to create a tiny object to float around the Earth. "What is that? A mini planet?" asked Sol.

"I call it a Moon. It will allow sunlight to pass thought it, so that night can be illuminated without it being daytime as well as letting some heat in!" explained Lun.

Stone's brows raised. "Just when I think you couldn't surprise us anymore today, Little Brother," he said. Aqueon added, "We should put moons on all the planets."

"That will take forever" said Stone.

"Oh nonsense!" said The Existence, "Watch this!" With a clap of his hands, a surge of giant meteors gravitated around the various planets. The meteors circled around them in suspension. Jupiter was so big, about seventy-nine moons gravitated around it. Sol and Fyreon's planets did not get moons, but that suited them just fine because they were jealous of Lun's idea anyway.

"Father! That was amazing! Could you teach me to do that?" asked Stone in absolute shock.

"Maybe later my child, let's get back to Earth!" said the Lord.

Umbra and Sol came to an agreement of twelve hours of day and twelve hours of night (with loopholes in this agreement). Upon shaking each other's hands, half the Earth was covered by night and the other by daylight. Lun focused and tethered his Will to the moons by holding hands with his siblings. A surge of energy flowed through him. After this, The Existence gently nudged Lun and asked, "I think you know what comes next, don't you, Son?"

"Um, life?" responded Lun.

"Good! Now watch your old man get to work!" said The Existence.

With a mere thought, trees emerged from the ground. Fish swam and leapt out of the water and back into the oceanic abyss. Animals of small and large stature walked from the forests and looked in their direction. Small insects fluttered in the breeze. One landed on Fyreon and she swatted it. A small fizzle was heard from the force of her smack. Mountains, hills, and fields expanded upon the landmass. The Existence was at peace and in his best mood when he created. "Hmm . . . this all looks nice, but it is still missing something," said The Existence.

He grasped a handful of mud near the ocean and created a humanoid sculpture from it. He fashioned arms and legs, then the torso, and finally, a face with eyes, nose, ears, and a mouth. The form was in the shape of man, much like the other Titians except for Aqueon. Father inspected his work and was satisfied, so he breathed the breath of life into the mud sculpture. Its muddy composition changed to flesh. The newly made man collapsed to the ground and began breathing. He lifted his head up to see the Titans.

"What is that?" asked Fyreon.

"A new Titan?" asked Sol.

"Why is it always boys? Why can't Fyreon and I have another sister?" said Aqueon with a groan.

"Clearly it is some sort of advanced animal . . . right, Father?" asked Stone.

"No. This is Man. He shall inhabit this world alongside the plants and animals," said the Lord. "Arise, Man," said Father. Man stood to his feet and patiently waited. "M-Man?" said the man. He was of tanned complexion, brown hair, brown eyes. He was pretty small compared to the Titans, but taller than Lun.

"Yes, that is your name. Now come, we have plans we must discuss," said the Lord. Man simply nodded and still seemed pretty confused—as were the Titans.

They walked through the Garden of Eden. The Existence explained to Man that Eden was Man's to rule. He was also to claim dominion over the plants and animals of Earth. Man was to be a just and fair ruler to these things. Man seemed to understand and began to interact with the flora and fauna of the land. He gave names to many plants and animals, from the tiniest creature to the largest. But he soon began to tire of being the only one of his kind. The Lord noticed this and put Man into a deep slumber.

He took a set of ribs from Man and fashioned a feminine humanoid sculpture, the form resembling Aqueon.

"A girl?" asked Aqueon.

"Yes. This was always a part of my plan, my child. I waited so long to do this to teach you the lesson of patience. Good things will come to those who wait. Alas, my heart began to weep at Man's plight as the only human." The Lord once again breathed the breath of life into this sculpture and she drew her first breath. "Arise, Woman, you are the opposite of Man, known as Woman. You shall be his equal and rule this land alongside him," said the Lord. "Awaken, Man," commanded the Voice of the Lord.

Man's eyes immediately opened; he felt no pain from having a set of ribs removed. He noticed the beautiful figure of Woman and he smiled, to which Eve returned by smiling back. "Hello, I am Man," he said. "Hello, I am Woman," said Woman, still smiling. And so, Man and Woman eventually fell in love and all seemed well; the world was at peace. However, the Adversary snuck into the Garden and seduced the humans into partaking of forbidden knowledge. The Lord was forced to banish them from the paradise because they now knew of Good and Evil. But things were not all too bad for the humans; the Lord still loved them as he did his own children and continued to guide them despite their mistake.

Chapter 9

After the Fall of Man occurred, the Primordial Titans became fascinated with the Earth and its little inhabitants. Civilizations began to form from the descendants of Man and Woman. However, the conflicts of Humanity began to take their toll on the Titan family. Lun was once again the Titan of Nothing—the smallest of the family. The bullying resumed once again and Lun became fed up with his family.

"You are overstepping on our agreement again, Brother! Did you forget?!" asked Sol.

"Sorry, Brother, I didn't mean to overstep. Won't happen again," said Umbra while reading a book. It was a compilation of stories of the descendants of Man and Woman.

Sol snatched the book and threw it far away. His eyes were glowing, "You always say that! This is the fourth time this MONTH!"

Umbra stood up and replied, "Like you're any better! You're always overstepping too, you hypocrite!"

Lun stood between his brothers, "Please stop fighting! We can work this out without relying on our fists!" he pleaded.

"Oh, shut up, Lun. You were the one who was supposed to keep nightfall and daytime separate and you can't even manage that. And another thing, I'm sick of hearing about wisps flying out of humans when they die!" yelled Sol.

"Stop yelling at Lun! Let's face it! You're just as guilty of over-stepping as I am. I'm sick of hearing they needed an additional hour for their crops. You and I know damned well that hour makes no difference! You know it, I know it, Lun knows it, even Father knows it, you greedy asshole!" said Umbra. Darkness swirled throughout his body.

Sol threw a ball of searing light at Umbra, burning the side of his face. Umbra growled as the wound was quickly patched and healed by darkness. He stabbed Sol in the eye with one of his tendrils, but the wound was quickly healed by light. Sol was glowing with anger. The Light Titan and Darkness Titan were about to fight.

Lun felt an energy within himself—and summoned up his will and yelled, "ENOUGH!" This action shocked the two Titans, they were unable to break free from Lun's power. Lun's eyes were brimming with a blue power. Lun was shocked by this power himself and let them go. Lun said, "I'm sick of this stupid bickering over day and night! As the youngest of this family, I'm ashamed to see the OLDEST of this family act like tiny human children over nothing. I'm done with it all. You know what? I'd rather live amongst the humans than spend another moment listening to this. Goodbye, Brothers." Lun then dove down to Earth, taking on a human form.

Lun landed face first into the dirt. The young Titan wiped and beat dirt from his body. He gained his bearings and realized where he was: a forest near a civilization. He looked at his reflection in the water and steadily adjusted himself as necessary to resemble a regular human: brown hair, brown eyes, tanned skin. However, in this human form, he was still very short much to his dismay. Lun then willed a blue tunic and matching cloak with moon patterns on the ends of it.

"Lun?" said the voice of the Lord. Lun said nothing before The Existence said, "Lun, this is your Father. Why did you leave home?"

"I'm sick of being the smallest. I'm sick of Umbra. I'm sick of Sol. I'm sick of all my siblings treating me like garbage even after I forgave them. So, I've decided to live amongst the humans for now. I refuse to return, not as I am, not as the Titan of Nothing. I must find who I am meant to be, my purpose, the reason why you created me," said Lun.

"I see. Very well then, this may be good for you, my Son. Just do not fall prey to sin. Be wise," said the Lord. Lun was surprised by his response and felt the presence of the Lord leave him.

It was nighttime, Lun heard the beating of drums and singing; he assumed it was another celebration by the humans for something. Food, music, and alcohol were the best way to describe these celebrations. Lun walked to the village and a few humans gave him some stares. Most eyed the unique patterning of his cloak.

"Greeting traveler," said a man of about forty, his beard streaked with grey.

"Hello," said Lun in passing. He was stopped by the man's thick, callused hand. "I don't want any trouble," said Lun. He moved the man's hand away.

"Too bad, because trouble came looking for you, outsider," said the man, his breath reeking of alcohol. He threw a punch at Lun with his massive fist. Lun avoided it by ducking. Lun raised up his fists but the drunkard kicked him so hard it sent the young Titan tumbling to the ground. The drunk furiously beat Lun, kicking him while he was down. Lun's body ached all over from the force of the blows. Human forms were not very sturdy. The man began to laugh. "Not going to fight back? This is no fun for me. C'mon, I'll even let you get a punch in."

"Father, stop! This boy did nothing to you!" pleaded a young lady. She was as pretty as she was kind. She tugged at her father's arm but to no avail.

The man pulled his arm away and said, "Away with you, Faith! I do as I please!" He viciously smacked his daughter across the face, knocking her aside. Lun's eyes glowed blue with fury. He lifted his hand and the drunkard flew about ten feet into the air. He fell into a chicken coop. Lun's voice echoed, "You are unworthy of the title of 'Father' if that's the way you treat your children, you pile of refuse." The drunk lumbered to his feet and ran away screaming. The drummers stopped, probably alerted by the screaming of Faith's idiot father. Lun approached Faith. Her face was bruised by her father's powerful blow. Lun extended his hand to her and asked, "Are you all right? Faith, was it?"

Faith warily looked and took Lun's hand. He helped her up. She pushed him hard, knocking him to the ground as she made her escape. He was seized by the arm by another man. Long hair dropped over his shoulders. He had brown eyes, tanned skin, and an earring made of bone. In his other hand, he held a spear and wore a brown armored tunic. Lun wondered if he was a guard or a soldier of some sort. Then more, similarly dressed, men began to surround him with their spears. One of them hit him over the head with a club, knocking him unconscious.

When he became somewhat conscious, he was being carried over the shoulder of one of the men until he passed out again. SPLASH! The Titan was awakened by the sensation of cold water being dumped on his head. He was in a chair, his wrists bound by rope to the armrests. Lun focused forward and there was a man in front of him. His hair was balding at the top, a flowing mane at the sides—a greying white color. A bone was skewered thorough his nose and wrinkles permeated throughout his face, a lifetime of experience. His harsh-looking eyes looked at Lun for a very long time. The silence was finally broken when he asked, "Who are you? Or rather, what are you?"

"Huh?" said Lun with a confused expression.

"You come to my village and attacked one of my people. One of my favored soldiers no less. Be you a foul demon? I shall ask once more and only once more," said the old man. He pulled a dagger from its sheath and put it to Lun's throat, "What. Are. You?"

Lun nervously replied, "I am called Lun. I am a Primordial Titan."

"A Primordial Titan? You? So puny and weak, like a frail boy. Why does the Great Text make no mention of you, 'Lun?'" said the old man.

"Are you telling me that your Great Text makes no mention of the Primordial Titans . . . or the Forbidden Ones?"

The old man quickly put his hand over Lun's mouth and shouted, "DO NOT SPEAK OF THE FOBIDDEN ONES!" He warily looked around and in grave tone stated, "Speaking of them brings no good, only evil into the hearts of Men. The mere utterance of those names . . . wreaks death and destruction."

"I've never read this Great Text," said Lun.

"Then clearly you are a demon. For you know it holds power against the likes of you." The old man pulled the knife away from his throat. He stepped back and said, "The village will decide your fate tomorrow, demon. Johal, the soldier you attacked, will be testifying against you. Rest. Because your death is apparent," said the old man. He left Lun in the cell, all tied up.

"Father, please help?" thought Lun. But there was no response, no presence. Lun was truly alone.

And so, he sat there in thought. That Johal character was clearly going to lie. That old man (who Lun presumes to be the Chief) was a loon. And he was tied up and expected to sleep. Surprisingly, Lun did eventually tire. Only humans get tired . . .

the weight of his current form felt real. Lun dozed off and was awakened to the shining of sunlight. A guard unlocked his cell and undid his bindings. Only to redo them with his wrists in front of his body now. Another guard came in and they escorted the Titan to the middle of the village. Angry clamoring and hateful stares greeted him. A table stood next to the execution stone laid nearby. Dried blood caked the stone.

The Chief slammed down his ceremoniously decorated staff, willing a large gust of wind at the crowd. They fell silent and the Chief yelled, "Silence! We are to begin trial of this accused demon. Arrested for the use of a blue force to knock Johal into the air several feet. Had he not run, Johal believes that he would have been killed. What say you to these accusations, demon?" said the Chief.

"Not guilty! He attacked me. Do you not see the injuries on my body? What I have done, I only did in self-defense! Can we trust the words of a man who is low enough to hit his own daughter for trying to quell his drunken rage?" pleaded Lun.

"You leave my daughter out of this, demon! It was clearly you who caused the bruise on my daughter's cheek! I would never strike her!" said Johal. Faith hid her face from the look of her father.

"If it is the truth you say, why not let Faith speak? If you are not the filthy liar you claim not to be?" said Lun.

Johal growled and said, "Is she not plagued enough at the sight of you, demon?"

"Enough," interjected the Chief. "Bring Faith forward." Faith was brought to the middle of the crowd. Her eyes nervously looked back to her Father, who slowly shook his head. The Chief looked at her patiently and asked, "Is what your father speaks the truth, Faith?"

Faith nervously replied, "Yes. I mean, no. I mean—"

The Chief raised his hand and calmly said, "You have nothing to fear, child. Speak the truth. No harm shall come to you."

Faith took a breath and winced as she spoke the truth, "That man . . . was attacked by my father, lost in a drunken stupor as he normally does during festival time. I tried to stop him, but my father smacked me to the ground. Then the mysterious man's eyes began to glow blue and with a motion of his hand, he launched the large figure of my father into the air. He landed in the chicken coop and ran. Then the man helped me up and asked if I was okay. But I was scared and so I pushed him and ran."

The Chief looked her in the eyes and said, "Look me in the eyes. Is this the absolute truth?" Faith nodded her head.

The Chief nodded and looked at the crowd, "Tell me, my people. Is this the first time Johal sinned, making an ass of my Guard?"

One brave man stepped forward. "Chief Is'kah, I must confess. The confession of Johal's daughter . . . it moved me. I must speak the truth as well. Johal abuses his power, drinks in excess, and I hear whispers of his other . . . misdeeds."

Then a woman came forth and said unto Is'kah, "He has stolen from us, robbing my husband and me of a portion of our crops. He once threatened to kill my husband if we did not obey."

Then another confessed, and another, and another. Lun felt an overwhelming force and it was clear that it was acting on the crowd somehow, moving them to tell the truth.

Johal injected, "They are lying! All of them!"

"All of them, Johal? You must think I am a fool. Guards, take this disgrace away; we shall deal with him later. Free the accused," said Chief Is'kah. The Guards nodded and undid Lun's bindings and took Johal by the arms away.

The Chief gestured with his head to Lun and said, "I believe you are innocent of this crime. Perhaps of others I do not know. Leave my village and never return."

Lun nodded and started moving through the crowd of people. He reflected on how odd this all was . . . and it bothered him. Lun left as instructed, but then he looked behind him.

Faith was running behind him! "Wait!" she yelled and so Lun stopped. She caught up to him and regained her breath. She asked, "How did you do that? What spell did you cast on the crowd?"

"What do you mean? I didn't cause that. At least I don't think I did, anyway," said Lun.

"Of course, you did! I never would have been brave enough to go against my Father like that," said Faith.

"That did not seem to stop you last night," replied Lun.

"I—well, that was different; he had no right to beat you like that. He hasn't been the same since my mother died," said Faith in a solemn tone. She sat on a rock and Lun sat on the ground next to her. They looked at the outskirts of the village.

"I'm sorry for your loss," said Lun.

"Not your fault, it was a demon that took her life. A horrible, evil one. It attacked our village. They always attack at night. Too cowardly to fight during the day," said Faith.

I wonder what Sol would say if he heard that right now, thought Lun to himself. "So, tell me more about these demons. What are they?" asked Lun.

Faith let out a gasp and said, "You seriously do not know?! The Great Book makes mention of them."

Lun shook his head and asked, "What is this Great Book all about?"

Faith said, "Very well, I will tell you what I know. The Great Book is an ancient text passed over the generations by my village. It speaks of the Fall of Man, the serpent's deception, and the birth of Nephilim, another name for the demons. When the son of Man, Cain, killed his brother Abel, he was cursed by The Existence. He is the Patriarch of the Nephilim. Man's second son Seth, born after Abel, became the Patriarch of Humanity. The Lord gave a scribe knowledge of this in the form of the Great Book to prepare humanity for the future. It also speaks of a time when The Existence's children shall lead us into a new era," said Faith, "I am surprised your parents never taught you of this or Nephilim."

"Well I only have one parent. And he never made mention of this all to us," said Lun.

"One parent? Was one of your parents killed as well?" asked Faith.

"Um, it's a bit more complicated than that. Regardless, you should head back to your village—if it is as dangerous as you say at night. You should be able to make it back by nightfall," said Lun.

"There is nothing for me there. Only a farm with crops that barely grow, no family who cares for me, and a dissatisfaction with my own life" said Faith.

"Do you intend to follow me?" said Lun.

Faith nodded. Lun sighed, "Very well. I suppose I could use a guide. Earth has changed much since my siblings and I last saw it."

Chapter 10

The Titans sat in silence. They observed their little brother Lun talking to Faith through a spherical projection. "This is all my fault. I shouldn't have been so hard on him," said Sol after he sighed.

"I'm not worried, I think this will be good for Lun," said Umbra, "Little man needs to toughen up."

Aqueon looked up from the sphere and said to them, "This never would have happened if you two weren't always bickering about your damned daytime and nighttime rules! Now you've driven him into the arms of this human!"

"Do not feign concern, Sister. You must accept your part in driving him away as well, always underestimating him. As have I," said Stone while he adjusted his spectacles.

Lun and Faith laughed over a joke that he told her.

"Humans are interesting creatures, but they find the smallest things amusing," said Aeolian. He took a bite of an apple. Fyreon said nothing but watched her little brother interact with the human. After a while, she walked out. As soon as she was out of sight, she sat alone.

While the Titans argued, the Lord sat in his chambers. He thought to himself, *Be wise and forever in my care, my Son.*

The next morning, Lun and Faith set out to what she described as the city of Aginoth. "Tell me more of this place—it is what you humans call a 'city?'" asked Lun.

"Yes, Aginoth is a large hub where humans from all over gather. Many kinds of people live there. I visited many times before with my mother," said Faith.

"I see. How long will it take us to get there?" asked Lun.

"Without an effective means of travel—perhaps a few days' time? Plus, there is the matter of food and drink . . . of which I brought little," Faith nervously chuckled.

"I do not require food, drink, or sleep like humans do," said Lun.

"Then explain why you were so hard to wake up this morning? I could have sworn I was shaking a rock," said Faith.

"As I said, we Titans do not REQUIRE these things, but they are wonderful to experience," said Lun. Then he saw a shimmering force of blue energy. "There is much mana in this area—it's so abundant," said Lun.

"Mana? What's that? I see nothing," asked Faith.

"Take a hold of my shoulder" said Lun.

Faith did as commanded and she was greeted to a shocking sight, "What is this? It is so beautiful!"

"As I said before, it is mana. The energy of all things; we Titans can sense it all around us," said Lun.

"Oh! So, you're like a bunch of mages?" asked Faith.

"Mages?" asked Lun.

"They are spoken about in the Great Text. Mages, or magi, are humans who can perform amazing feats using mana. I never imagined it would look so pretty. Magi are said to be descended from Nephilim, but not all of them are evil. Some choose to use their abilities for good," explained Faith.

Lun thought to himself, "Great feats? I wonder…" Lun began to concentrate on the mana. He put both of his hands toward the mana and much to his surprise, it listened! He and Faith were lifted into the air in a chariot made of pure mana. It was an azure-colored construct.

"Oh, my goodness! This is amazing!" shouted Faith.

"It actually worked!" said Lun.

"Have you never done this sort of thing before?" asked Faith. "I've seen my siblings do it before. I never seemed able to do it before. I wonder if I can get it to move," said Lun. He concentrated as hard as he could on the chariot. The chariot flew at an insane speed across the sky. Faith and Lun held on the chariot as tight as they could. They made it to the city of Aginoth in the span of a few hours.

"That was insane! We made it here so quickly!" said Faith. "So how do we get down to the ground again?" asked Faith.

"Um, I didn't really think that far ahead," responded Lun. They were several feet in the air. "Let me try this," said Lun as he put a hand on the chariot. He closed his eyes and focused. He slowly brought the cart down in front of the city. It descended down gracefully. but at the last second, the chariot phased out of existence! The duo fell onto the ground, Faith landing on top of Lun. "Well that could have gone smoother," said Lun.

"Yeah, you think?" replied Faith. The two got up and dusted themselves off.

The city of Aginoth was several times larger than the village. Its buildings were made of carved stone of varied sizes and shapes. Children played in the marketplace. Merchants shooed the children away from their market stands. The stands were filled with various goods such as produce, weapons, and several oddities. A man performed "miracles" to the onlookers. He was a mage simply showing off his ability to cast fire, wind, and water from the ground. A few women were in an alleyway. They were very not-modestly clothed and beckoned Faith and Lun (but mainly Lun) over to them. Faith warned Lun not to go near those women. She whispered in his ear, "They're prostitutes."

"What do prostitutes do?" asked Lun. Faith whispered to Lun of their profession. Lun turned bright red and said, "Oh my."

Faith took Lun by the hand and guided him to another part of the city. They walked to a temple devoted to The Existence, Bearers of Faith. "Elahi?!" yelled Faith. The priest turned around and said, "Faith?! How have you been?!" He ran up to her hugged her graciously.

"I am well, Priest Elahi!" said Faith as she returned his hug. Elahi then noticed Lun and said to her, "Enjoying the married life?"

Faith blushed and replied, "No, no, no! Lun is not my husband, he is merely a friend. I have come to ask a favor of you, Your Holiness."

"Ah, one day you shall find the one for you. Well, come on then!" said Elahi. He gestured with his hand for Lun to come forth.

Lun shook Elahi's hand and said, "It is a pleasure to meet you; I am called Lun."

Elahi smiled, but it quickly diminished as soon as he sensed a presence emanating from Lun. He looked him in the eyes and then around the area. "Faith, I need to speak privately with you. Now," said Elahi.

"Excuse us a moment, Lun," said Faith as she walked to the Temple's private quarter.

Elahi asked, "Faith, do you not know who this is?"

Faith replied, "He is Lun, of course."

"No, he is more than that! I felt it, his presence. It is not human, otherworldly in a spiritual sense. I feel as though the Lord sent me a direct message to me, telling me that this is a Primordial Titan, one of His first creations. His son . . . what led him here?" asked Elahi.

"That I do not know. He claimed he left his home due to frustration with his family," said Faith.

"Fallen? As Jamaerah had fallen?!" asked Elahi.

"No, just taking a while from them to discover himself," said Faith.

"How can you be so certain he is merely here to 'get away' as you say?" said Elahi.

"By my namesake, I trust him. I will admit that he is not human but is certainly not here to harm us. Look at him! Do you think this man is capable of destruction?" said Faith. They peered out the window, and there was Lun. A butterfly gently landed on his finger. Then it landed on his face, causing Lun to sneeze.

Elahi looked back to Faith said, "Very well . . . if you trust him, then I shall put trust in you and your namesake with the Lord. Now what was this favor you require of me?"

"We are in dire need of a place to stay. We have no money, food, or drink. My father has been jailed and Lun is banished from my village."

Elahi sighed and then said, "Very well. I shall allow you both to stay the night." And so Lun and Faith were given host by Elahi for a time. Lun learned much of the city and its ways.

In addition to temples to the Existence, there were temples to false gods as well. These gods included Lun's siblings, The Forbidden Ones and Fallen Angels under different names. Lun heard rumors these pagan believers performed rituals consisting of orgies, sacrifices, and other things considered sinful to the Lord. These rituals were performed to appease their false idols in exchange for power, gold, and other vices. Elahi warned them both to stay away from these pagan Temples, but eventually

Lun's curiosity got the better of him. He snuck out one night and decided to visit the Temple of Hti'vad, once known as Davith. He was stopped from entering by a man wearing a loin cloth and a wolf skin over his head. After a moment, the man just stopped and Lun let in. People were prostrating themselves within the temple, often with severe lacerations to their bodies. The others were praying to a statue of a humanoid figure, built in the image of Davith's now-corrupt form.

Lun approached the leading priest, who wore a similar attire to the guard outside. "My Lord seeks audience with you," said the leading priest. His brown eyes turned to solid white and his body started to convulse violently. He then spoke in a voice that was not his own, "Hello Brother. I have watched you from afar."

Lun replied, "Are you Davith?"

"I am no longer called that. My name is now Hti'vad. I have seen you running around with that human, learning of their culture. Why have you come here?" said Hti'vad.

"I was curious . . . of why you were banished. Why there are temples built in your and my other exiled siblings' honor? I have so many questions, but Father refuses to answer them because they pain him greatly."

Hti'vad smiled and replied, "O Little One, there is much Father has not told you all. Take my hand and all shall be answered," said the possessed body. He was now bleeding from the eyes. Lun nervously stepped forward and took the hand. He was transported to the Void.

He was surrounded by the other Forbidden Ones, all in varied, nonsensical forms that are vaguely humanoid. They sat in thrones of their own design and the one in the middle beckoned to Lun—his throne built the highest. "Do not be afraid. Approach, Little Brother," said Hti'vad. A chair was conjured for Lun.

Scar-li-ho-mun said in his very gravelly voice, "So this is Father's replacement for us? So puny."

"Hush your tone, Scar-li-homun. This is still our Family; the Titans know not of Father's transgressions against us," said Hti'vad.

"Why do you all look this way?" asked Lun.

"We have resided in the Void for eons. No rules apply here like in the Universe. And our hatred for Father ran so deep, we chose to allow our hate to choose our forms," said Ithygriss, once known as Theosorh, Patron of Logic.

Nuipex caressed Hti'vad's face and then looked at Lun. She said, "Perhaps it would be better if we took more familiar forms. The Little One seems terrified. His wary look belies his fearfulness." And with that, their forms regressed into the forms known.

"So, you want answers?" said Vh'ela, "Then we shall give them to you."

"Long ago, when this existence was first created, the Lord had created the Universe. But soon he became tired of being lonely, and so he created us," started Hti'vad.

"And for a time, he loved us, and we loved him," continued Nuipex,

"However . . ." "We had a different view of how the Universe should be ordered. But Father did not agree with us, the arrogant fool," said Vh'ela.

"And so, we plotted to kill him . . . and to take his mighty throne," said Scar-li-homun. "But he overpowered us—and he decided rather than kill us, to banish us," said Aishidd'k.

"He closed his ears to our suffering—and left us to rot," said V'alko bitterly.

"We began to reach out to the humans by passing messages through the fallen angel Jamaerah, now branded the Adversary. He wanted the same things as us, but he never stood a chance against The Existence's might. But . . . with the faith of Father's own creations . . . we discovered a way back into the Universe," said Hti'vad.

"And what will you do with that power? And how do we fit into all of this?" asked Lun.

"Simple. Father wanted a replacement family, one more obedient to his will than we. Almost puppets to his will," said Hti'vad. He put a hand on Lun's shoulder. "What we seek . . . is the destruction of our Father, so we may usher in a new era for the Universe. A fairer, more just one where all, including the 'sinful' Nephilim can live amongst the humans. Where only the strong can thrive while the weak act as fodder for them!" said Hti'vad with a smile.

Lun sighed and then replied, "T-This is so much to take in. I—"

"You are just a puppet that Father pretends has actual feelings and morals," Hti'vad injected, "Sorry to say—but it is the truth and I must speak it. We could change all of that however."

Nuipex walked over and with a seductive smile said, "Simply join us. Join your power with ours. We could make you more than a puppet. Doesn't that sound wonderful? The melding of our bodies . . ." Nuipex kissed Lun on the mouth, to which Lun recoiled back in disgust. He exclaimed, "You are my sister! This is not right!"

"And who says that it is not right? Father? To Hell with him and his Law!" said Nuipex as she took on her hideous form. The others followed suit and surrounded Lun. "If you do not join us, we will take your body by FORCE. You are the weakest, you cannot fight back," said Hti'vad. He grabbed Lun with his tentacled appendages.

"I am NOT weak" said Lun as his eyes glowed blue with rage. He pushed all the Forbidden Ones back with a powerful force of energy.

They all grabbed him at once. "Cute, but you cannot take us all alone!" said Scar-li-homun.

"He isn't alone," said the familiar voice of Umbra.

The darkness of the Universe began to spread, pushing the Forbidden Ones back from Lun. Umbra picked up his brother and Sol fired shots of light at the Forbidden Ones. The Forbidden Ones screamed in indescribable roars. Umbra opened a portal to the Temple of the Lord, where Lun was greeted by all his siblings in human forms. "Why the hell would you talk to the Forbidden Ones?!" yelled Umbra.

This must be serious if Umbra is yelling. He hardly ever yells, thought Lun.

"Do you not realize how dangerous they are? They are banished from this existence for a reason!" said Aqueon. She hugged him very tightly.

"What are you all doing here?" asked Lun as he hugged his sister back.

"We have been watching you from afar. We were worried the second you left Paradise to reside on Earth," said Fyreon.

"Dad's not too happy about us intervening but at the same time was subtly encouraging us to save you. You know how he is with his mysterious way of talking sometimes," said Aeolian.

Faith ran outside, spear in hand, and yelled, "Lun!"

She stopped in her tracks when she saw the Primordial Titans with Lun. They were dressed in standard clothing and their forms were generic human forms at best. "Who are you?! Have you come to attack Lun?!" said Faith, wielding the spear.

"Faith, stop! These are my siblings!" said Lun. He stood in front of them.

"Aww, she thinks that spear can hurt us," said Aeolian to Aqueon.

Elahi came out to see and said, "What is the commo—" Elahi stopped in his tracks. He had the same sensation when he first met Lun. He nearly fainted until Umbra caught him.

Faith put down the spear and asked, "Why are they all here?"

"That is a good question; why are you all here besides saving me?" asked Lun.

"We should probably discuss this inside," said Stone. People were staring. They all went inside the Temple's private chambers.

They sat and Umbra explained what was going on. "So, you all know how I was created from the darkness of the ever-expanding Universe right?" They nodded in agreement. "Well, what you all don't know is that I also act as a seal to the outside of the Universe. To keep our 'dear' siblings out. And believe me, they tried. For eons. I can feel it. This 'faith' that these pagans have been giving them has given them significant power. All seven of them. And . . . it's only a matter of time before they get here," explained Umbra.

"At first Father was just going to let Lun here run around and make his own choices to find himself, but we don't have that time anymore," said Sol, "He told us your purpose Lun…it's very important."

Lun asked, "I'm . . . important?"

"Yes. VERY important," said Aqueon.

"Well? Out with it!" said Lun.

"Well the thing is . . ." droned Aeolian. "You're a weapon," said Fyreon.

Chapter 11

"I'm a weapon? What does that mean?" asked Lun.

Umbra said, "We're the seals, you're the backup, simply put. Lun . . . you're not the Titan of Nothing. You're actually the Titan of Spirit."

Faith asked, "Spirit? You mean as in ghosts and specters?"

"Well that and more; he is the motivation that drives humans. He is that emotional spur. He is anger, sorrow, happiness, and everything that makes living beings more than an automaton of flesh," said Stone.

"Tch, lucky bastard," said Fyreon.

Lun was at a loss, "I-I'm . . . my purpose?"

"You were created from the Lord's Will, more specifically you're like an upgraded version of Metatron. You know how he is simply an extension of the Lord? You are like that but given independence. Father gains power from his thoughts. You gain yours from your emotion. He created you in case Jamaerah and the Forbidden Ones decided to directly come here and wreak havoc on humanity."

"I think that your coming here was no coincidence either," said Sol.

"Are you saying Father used me?" said Lun.

"No Lun, he wanted you to realize for yourself why you must fight. To find your Reason . . ." said Umbra.

Lun began to cry, "Why . . . why did he not tell me from the beginning if he knew? Why did he lie to me? I don't understand . . ."

Faith said, "The Lord works in mysterious ways . . ."

"You got that right," said Lun as he jerked away from her and ran outside.

Faith and Lun's siblings gave chase. "Lun, wait!" said Sol. Lun flew up high and landed on the Moon.

"Where did he go?!" asked Faith with worry and shock.

"To the Moon. It's where he likes to be alone and think sometimes," said Aqueon.

Lun sat on the moon, looking at the Earth and began to sob. "Why? Why, Father? Why did you keep this a secret from me?" yelled Lun to himself.

"To help you understand," echoed the voice of the Lord.

"Understand what? How it feels to be weak and helpless? To have the strong regard you as worthless trash?" sobbed Lun.

"As cruel as this may sound . . . yes," said the Lord. He finally appeared to Lun in a white robe.

He sat next to his son and Lun asked, "Why?" He wiped the tears from his face.

"Think about it. How do you think those humans would feel if they realized your power?" asked The Existence.

"Like how I felt?" asked Lun.

"Now think of this, the Firstborn think of themselves how Fyreon would think of you before you came into your own. Very proud of you by the way for that," said The Existence with a smile.

"I see . . . but I don't get how I am a weapon. Just because I can control mana like a mage doesn't make me some ultimate weapon," said Lun.

"Oh, my child, how you doubt yourself," said The Existence. He lightly touched Lun's head and they were transported to another place instantly. They were on Mars.

A Martian was waiting there for them. They were a thin humanoid shape, had red eyes, orange skin, and wore clothing of wonderous shades and symbols on them. This one wore a magnificent crown of fire. "My Lord, has Creator Lun realized his destiny?" asked the crowned Martian.

"He has, King Oram," said The Existence. King Oram nodded and spoke in a Martian language to his subjects. They nodded back and began to prepare a place for them. "Whoa, they've . . . changed so much," said Lun.

"Indeed. Be proud. Don't worry, I've been keeping an eye on them for you in your absence," said the angel Vigil. He appeared next to them. "A ship has been prepared, my Lord," said King

Oram, who bowed. They entered a starship, which flew them over a beautiful Martian civilization.

It flew to an open knoll and The Existence gestured to Lun, "Put your hand to the ground like this."

Lun nodded and the ground resonated with his touch. His palm became highlighted and connected to a large grid on the ground. The grid slowly rose up to reveal a metal temple made of a blue substance. There were moon and star patterns all over it. "What is this place?" asked Lun.

"It is your Space. I prepared it for you long ago," said the Lord.

Lun walked down it and discovered the immense chamber. Mana flowed as if it were water there. It began to shoot out like water as Lun walked forward. At the end of the massive hall was a pod. It pulsated and glowed as Lun approached. He touched it and the pod opened, revealing an armor made of a unique alloy: It moved and pulsed like tissue, yet it was somehow a mana-infused alien metal. Alongside that was a blade of fine alien alloys. It was far different from traditional steel or some other earthly metal. The armor shook before finally firing itself at Lun! It forcibly attached itself to him. The blade moved towards him but stopped short of his face by the grip. Lun grabbed the sword and his eyes glowed and pulsed with knowledge: knowledge of himself.

Chapter 12

"THE MOON?!" yelled Faith, "Why are you all standing here with no purpose?! Bring him down this instant if he's important as you say!"

"We can't. Father's orders," said Umbra.

"He intends to train Lun on Mars," said Aqueon.

"Mars? What is this Mars?" asked Faith.

"It is a world that Lun created; its people are much more advanced there. Their technology will help us in the oncoming battle against the Firstborn," said Stone.

Faith attempted to respond but she could not think of what to say. "Please try to understand. This is beyond you. We need him. There is no time to waste on emotions," said Fyreon.

Faith put her head down and said, "I've known Lun for a few years now, I care about him. I'm worried. What if . . ."

"Don't worry about the if. Know this. You want to help? Have your namesake in him," responded Umbra.

Elahi said, "Is the Existence punishing us for mortal sin?"

"No. This is more than that. It's a family dispute and the First-born are choosing to involve you in it," responded Umbra.

A crashing of the gate was heard nearby. Several pagans wielding magic and weapons came crashing through. "And here's trouble," said Aeolian.

Stone slammed the ground with his fists and erected a much more solid wall with spikes at the top. These spikes impaled a few of the invading pagans. Fyreon burned a group of pagans to cinders using her flame. Aqueon willed water to her and drowned several of them. Umbra impaled a few of them with his tendrils of darkness. Sol outright blew up the remaining by overcharging them with light.

"It is not safe here. Elahi and Faith, you must leave this place," said Umbra.

"Take us with you!" said Faith, holding onto Umbra's cloak.

"We Titans are not supposed to—" Umbra paused for a moment, ". . . okay, Father," said Umbra as he summoned a portal to another place.

Lun walks out of the temple, shining in his flesh-like armor. "You look good, Son. How does it feel?" asked The Existence.

"It feels right, like I was meant to wear this," said Lun.

"You are," said Vigil, "It is your destiny to become a beacon to life, the Spirit of the Universe."

"I am the Titan of Sprit . . . what does that entail exactly?" asked Lun.

"Come to me and I will show you," said The Existence with an outstretched hand. He patiently awaited his son's approach. Lun did as commanded and he grasped his father's hand.

A sudden pulse unlocked within Lun's mind. He saw himself. A blue energy emanated around him. Wisps, specters, and other spirits swirled around him. They spoke to him, their touch flowed with memories of their lives and skills. Lun saw him proficiently using the elements of his siblings as well as his own power of spirit. Holographic copies of various weapons such as swords, shields, and other machinations took form around him. He sensed his connection to the Moon and realizes its purpose. "I see . . . now I understand. But I still do not understand why you did not reveal this all to me sooner. And what of Faith, Elahi, and my Siblings? Are they okay?" said Lun.

"They are fine. They're in Paradise after being attacked by worshippers of the Firstborn," answered the Lord.

"Oh no! Faith and Elahi are dead?!" said Lun with urgency.

"No, no. I have merely granted them asylum into Paradise for now. Their souls remain in their flesh. King Oram," said the Lord.

"Yes, my Lord?" said the King.

"We are taking our leave for now. Are your weapons ready? I sense that the Seal within my son Umbra is weakening," said the Lord.

"We are ready, my Lord. We will give them no reprieve for their misdeeds," said the Martian King. Several armor-clad Martian soldiers came afoot armed with rifles and blades unlike anything seen before.

"Good. Let us fight a good battle and be victorious," said The Existence. He, Vigil, and Lun faded out of existence on the red planet. They now were in Paradise.

"L-Lun!" said one of the angels in surprise of seeing the young Titan.

"That armor looks amazing!" said another angel, the lesser angels begin to surround Lun, Vigil, and The Existence.

"Now, now, little ones. The Lord and Lun have things to discuss. A battle is forthcoming—rally the other angels. We must prepare," said Vigil as he flew up with the other angels.

"I'm surprised I was missed so much up here," said Lun.

"Of course, you were. The minute you decided to live amongst the humans, I missed you greatly," said The Existence. The Existence opened his throne room. Faith and the other Titans looked in Lun and the Lord's direction.

"Lun!" said Faith as she ran toward him and hugged him tightly.

Lun smiled and hugged her back. "I'm sorry for running off like that."

"Never mind that; I'm glad that you are safe. What is that armor you're wearing? It's . . . unlike anything I've ever seen before," said Faith as she looked at Lun's armor.

"It is of Martian design; nothing on Earth comes even close to its intricate design," said the Lord. Faith looked upon the massive figure of the Lord and got down on her knees, as did Elahi in his presence.

"T-The Lord?! I-I . . . forgive me. I am unworthy to look upon you," said Elahi.

"I . . . I can't believe this. I'm in the same room as The Existence! I-I . . ." said Faith.

The Lord smiled and said to them, "I am grateful for your fealty to me and even more grateful to the both of you for looking after my son Lun for me. Arise, you have both earned that." Faith and Elahi do as commanded. Lun gently tugged on The Existence's robe and whispered in his ear, "Father, could I . . . talk to Faith alone for a moment? Just the two of us?" The Existence nodded and gave them a private chamber to talk. Lun and Faith sat down on the bench.

"So . . . you're an actual Titan. Like an honest, genuine Primordial Titan," said Faith with a smile.

"Yes. And I realized my purpose. I'm not just a weapon. I'm the Titan of Spirit," responded Lun.

"And what does that mean? Are you a ghost?" said Faith.

"No . . . I simply control them as well as am the driving force of living beings. I am the Will that moves them to action, I am the energy and the spark that gives passion, I am all of this and more," said Lun.

"Tch, whatever. You'll always be plain old Lun to me," said Faith with a smirk.

"Oh, come now. Admit it. It's amazing. Most humans must die to even get to Paradise. And you're still in your flesh. I bet Elahi is freaking out more about it than you though. You've always been an interesting human," said Lun.

Faith responded with, "And you've always been an interesting person. Much more than me . . ."

"No, you mean much more to me than a regular human," said Lun.

"What do you mean?" asked Faith.

Lun said, "Well . . . I mean, I've known you for a few years now. And . . . I think I understand what love is like finally. It only seems to happen when . . . I'm around you."

Faith said, "I . . . wow, that's . . . I don't know what to say."

Lun smiled and said, "I figured I should tell you since I am going to battle against my older Siblings. I may not survive. So many lives at stake and I am more than willing to take the risk. Especially since yours is at stake. I don't know what I would do if anything happened to you."

Faith suddenly kissed Lun, to which he returned. Lun smiled at Faith. They left the chamber and joined the others.

Umbra felt a pounding headache. He groaned as his eyes began to glow. "Umbra, are you all right?!" said Sol.

"T-They're coming! I don't know how long I can hold them!" said Umbra, who was now on his knees in pain.

"What do you see in the Void, Brother?" asked Stone.

"I see . . . I see . . .! Their army!" The white void was filled with various Nephilim as the Forbidden Ones and their lumbering forms traveled behind them. The Nephilim were crashing against the gates. Umbra was in so much pain.

"Let them in," said Lun. "I will be the first thing that greets them. Half of you defend the planets; the others come with me."

Chapter 13

Umbra groaned as he was unable to suppress the horde of Nephilim any longer. Lun, Sol, and Fyreon awaited the massive army. Sol and Fyreon willed their attire to something more combat-worthy: plated armor of the respective colors of gold and red. The Nephilim were of varying sizes. Some resembled humans, others, the fallen angels, and the rest were outright beasts. In front of them was a man of great stature, easily about eight feet or more. He rode a ten to twelve-foot steed with eight legs. He wore black armor. Tattoos and scars covered his body. In one hand, he held a spear which glowed with the energy of the Void.

"And so, these are the warriors that wish to stop us, Father?" yelled the man to the mass known as Hti'vad.

"We shall not falter, Pinnock, my Son. Do not fail me," said the Motivator of Betrayal.

"Losing? I do not intend on it. TO ARMS!" yelled General Pinnock. Several Ogre-like Entities came forth.

Fyreon sent a rain of flaming javelin amongst the Nephilim that aimed their bows and arrows at her. Several fell, but Pinnock simply blocked the volley using his shield. It was also covered in this Void-like substance. "The left side! Join me in attacking Earth and Mars! Heralt! To Mars! Beland! Demolish these inferior Titans . . ." ordered Pinnock as he willed portals onto Earth and Mars. He leaped into the Earth portal and was followed by a portion of his troops. Lun willed the spirits of the fallen and used them to attack against the horde before they can get farther into the universe. Sol landed onto the invisible bridge and summoned a blade of light. He slashed and tore through archers. Fyreon gave Sol backup by flying overhead and blasting the ones that attempted to attack him. Suddenly, several harpies attacked Fyreon and she was knocked to the ground. She covered her body in flames and they were burnt to cinders.

On Mars, Heralt and his horde of para-soldiers invaded— harpies and sylphs, and other creatures of lore. King Oram raised his blade of crimson energy and commanded his troops in their Martian language. A few soldiers fired anti-air laser technology which severely crippled the onslaught. The Martian King easily slashed and tore through their numbers. His tall nimble body was almost like a weapon itself. Heralt charged toward the King with a powerful weapon of the Void. He prayed to the Forbidden Ones to grant him strength and charged an attack.

"Prepare the RAILGUN!" yelled King Oram to his soldiers. Outside of the outskirts of his kingdom, a massive alien laser rose from the ground. Several engineers pressed buttons and aimed—they charged up the laser.

"Foolish Martians . . . you cannot win against the Firstborn," said Heralt. He charged up with energy provided by the Forbidden Ones. He lunged right at the city with a kamikaze attack in mind. King Oram prayed to the Lord to protect his people and he charged at Heralt. With sheer strength alone, Heralt was held by Oram. He did not let go, and he ordered his people to fire. The railgun blasted Heralt, the troops of Heralt, and . . . King Oram into nothingness. The Martians were victorious—but at what cost?

On Earth, Nephilim of massive size such as ogres, trolls, and other giants tore apart human civilizations. Elves and gnomes swiftly moved about, killing the terrified survivors of the initial attacks. The troops quickly moved as a unit throughout the massive landmass.

They were stopped in the middle by Aqueon and Stone, who were clad in the respective colors of blue and tan. "This senseless slaughter comes to an end now. We will not let you to continue to destroy what was created here," said Stone with determination.

"How dare you be of human blood! How can you do this?" said Aqueon.

'Pinnock replied, "We may have their blood, but we are not humans. We are above them, just as the Firstborn are above their Father. Enough talk, let us fight!" The Nephilim General raised his spear and clashed with them both. Aqueon tore through several of Nephilim with freezing water. Stone impaled several of the Nephilim on metal spears conjured from the ground. Pinnock remained unharmed; the Void gave him power unlike that of the Titans. "You can't win! Submit and I may spare you as servants to my Father," said Pinnock arrogantly.

The Titans were overwhelmed and enacted a plan. Aqueon willed the entire ocean to her side. Stone willed the entire continent to his bidding. He split the entire continent apart into seven pieces and forced most of the troops on the continent Antarctica. Aqueon lashed out and dragged the remaining Nephilim into the sea. There were a few stragglers, but they ran away. They lost the will to fight. The ones on Antarctica froze to death. Pinnock drowned in the massive wave that wiped his troops away.

Back at the battle in the Void entrance, Lun and his siblings fiercely repelled what they could of the Nephilim. "Pinnock! My son! You will pay for this, Titans," yelled Davith. He and his brethren attempted to make their way through the portal. Only Davith broke free and he immediately tackled Lun. "You little fucking brat! How dare you oppose me?!" said Davith ferociously.

Lun responded by slamming Davith's head onto the bridge. Davith threw him away from the main battle. Fyreon and Sol continued to slay the remaining forces as Umbra worked on getting the portal closed again. Lun yelled, "I would rather die than see this Universe fall in your hands."

"Those terms are acceptable," said Davith as he willed a blade of the Void into his hand.

Chapter 14

Lun stood up against the elder brother Hti'vad, with blade in hand. The Firstborn gave a mighty punch which blew him away into the void of the Universe. "Fool, you cannot beat me in this world. You and all of the Titans shall fall . . . a shame you chose to stand by a man who abandoned us," said the eldritch being. The mass that he once had begun to take a more humanoid form. He was clad in armor of shimmering light and twirled the Void blade in his hand.

"I would never betray Father. He never gave up on you all, you know. You're just too stubborn to understand His Plan and why it must stay this way," said Lun as he withdrew his blade. It pulsed with the power of spirit.

"Lies . . . LIES!" yelled Hti'vad as he and Lun slashed against each other.

Lun's armor held up well against the attacks. Its fleshy-metallic covering took up much of the impact of the Void blade. Sol and Fyreon flew over to Lun, but Hti'vad willed tentacles from his back that flung them back several miles. Hti'vad gripped Lun with a tentacle. Lun broke out of it using a beam from his eyes, severing the appendage. The Firstborn recoiled back in pain and slid his open palm across the Void blade, covering it in his blood. He flung the Void-infused blood in the form of several flashes. Lun quickly put up his arms to erect a barrier in front of himself. The sphere shattered but he was able to endure the slashes. Lun willed several spirit arms wielding blades to his side and sent them at Hti'vad. The Firstborn easily slapped them away, but they boomeranged back at him. A couple of them pierced his hide.

Hti'vad rushed at Lun with his blade, and Lun easily blocked the attack with a barrier. But then the Firstborn disappeared behind him and easily broke through. He grabbed Lun by his head and flew over to the planets. In a repeating process, Hti'vad slammed his head into the planets. All the way from Pluto to Mercury. Finally, Hti'vad slammed him against the Earth's Moon, causing a massive crater to form. "You cannot win, our Father does nothing as you fight his battles for you. Because you are merely a tool to him. Nothing more," said the Firstborn. Lun started to laugh in response. "Ah, I finally broke your mind. Do you finally admit defeat? I may grant you a swift death," said Hti'vad.

"Ha, ha, ha! I have not lost my sense. I just found this amusing," said Lun.

"Amusing?" asked Hti'vad

"Because you're standing right where I want you," said Lun as he willed the gravity of the moon onto Hti'vad.

Lun unsheathed his blade again and lunged at Hti'vad. He easily parried the slash with his sword. He willed spirits from the Earth to hold on to and harass Hti'vad. As Hti'vad was distracted, Lun charged for an attack. Lun summoned the power of faith in the Existence around him: the excitement, anger, sorrow, and fear of the inhabitants of Earth. He glowed with mighty energy. Lun stabbed his sword into the ground of the Moon and positioned himself to blast the evil Forbidden One. Hti'vad was able to swipe away the specters and realized what he was doing. He grabbed Lun and threw him down to Earth. Lun kept focus. They fought in the air and the struggle ended with Lun throwing Hti'vad face first into Antarctica.

"Clever trick trying to use that planet against me. I suppose you are Father's most formidable weapon," said Hti'vad.

"That's not all I am. I am protector to all living beings. I am their Hate, I am their Happiness, I am all the energy that Drives people to action. And you are upsetting the peace," said Lun.

"Peace? Happiness? You truly are ignorant. These creatures fight with each other; they kill each other for power and profit. They are merely tools and nothing more," said Hti'vad.

"No. It is you who are ignorant. They are much more than their fury. Life is creative . . . it's beautiful. And it is part of His Plan," said Lun.

"I hope you made peace with Father, because you will never see him again," said the Firstborn. He pointed his blade at Lun.

He charged at the now weaponless Lun and Lun willed spectral blades to him once again. Hti'vad blasted them back as far as he could. Lun managed to wrestle the blade from Hti'vad and he kicked him back. He gathered more energy from the Moon and life energy from Mars and Earth. He took the Void blade and with a mighty slash, he slashed a portal back into the Void. The two begin to fight once more. Hti'vad gained the upper hand by willing a tentacle from his body. He stabbed Lun in the back with a dagger. But Lun wanted this—he pushed the fallen celestial back into the Void with his remaining energy. Hti'vad screamed as he was once again torn to pieces by the Void. He yelled, "This is not over, fool! You will not survive your wounds! You love this world so much, you can die on it!" Lun was taken to Paradise by The Existence, who finished obliterating the remaining attacking Nephilim in the universe.

"Lun!" said Faith as she took a hold of him. The Existence waved his hand over him and Lun's physical wounds slowly healed. "Hti'vad . . . he stabbed me with a Void dagger. I think the damage . . . goes beyond physical or spiritual," said Lun. He collapsed to the ground. His siblings surrounded him, as did angels. The angels carried him to a room for healing. "Son, I am the Lord. You will not die this day, I forbid it." Lun smiled as he began to lose consciousness. He was in a bed, surrounded by Faith and his family. "You are not leaving me . . . and I will not leave you," said Faith, her eyes welling up with tears.

Chapter 15

Lun was resting in the chamber with Faith sitting by his side. He was peaceful, his eyes were closed, and he slowly breathed. Faith removed his armor that coated him and placed him in more comfortable robes. New skin slowly regenerated over his old wounded flesh, but the wounds of his mind were still there. No matter how much they healed, they will always bounce back to him.

The Lord contemplated what to do, but he was wrought with emotions once again. "I cannot lose any more children, what am I to do?" said The Existence to Vigil.

"Uh, Lord? Is Lun going to be okay?" asked Faith.

The Existence lifted her up in his hand and said to her, "He is recovering, but it is unknown how long it will take him. It may be months, maybe even years. These time frames are different for us of course. Years to you are mere minutes to us. He may not even wake up for centuries," said the Lord.

"But what will the humans do? He's the Titan of Spirit after all. He cannot die; otherwise, what will happen to those spirits?" asked Stone.

"What a mess . . ." said Fyreon before she turned away to hide her tears.

"He saved us—despite all that we did to him," said Sol.

"I suppose this makes him the Biggest of us now," said Umbra. His head was bandaged, and his eyes no longer glowed.

Aeolian frowned, "I don't know how to feel . . . there's just an empty space in my heart."

Aqueon wiped away a few tears and said, "This is an unfortunate turn of events."

"Fear not, I am still with you all," echoed the voice of Lun. Everyone's expressions changed from solemn to that of shock.

"LUN?! How is this possible?!" asked Faith. He appeared before them in the form of a translucent apparition with a smile. "Are you dead?" she asked.

"No, merely having an out-of-body experience of sorts. My body is very weak . . . but my spirit is invincible. Obviously, I cannot be Earth's protector like this. I have a solution. Faith, I love you. But it is obvious that we can never be together in the way that I desire us to be. I have my Responsibility, and you have yours. So—I have decided to make you my Vessel," said Lun.

Aqueon scoffed, "Typical male. Almost on his deathbed and STILL trying his hardest to be in sinful union with a woman."

"Oh hush! I mean Faith will become the bearer of my power," said Lun's spirit.

"Or the bearer of his children . . ." whispered Sol to Umbra who snickered.

"Oh, shut up! Faith . . . come forth," said Lun.

Faith came face to face with him and he held her hands, "Close your eyes," said Lun. "What do you see?"

Faith said, "I see . . . you, your true form. It's . . . amazing. I—I'll gladly become your Vessel. I wish to protect humanity as you protected them. But . . . I want you. And only you," said Faith as Lun's Titan form loomed over her. Lun's aura willed itself to Faith. It tethered itself to her soul. Faith felt a rush of energy and it was done. She opened her eyes.

Lun caressed her check before kissing her passionately once more before fading away. "I know you do . . . but we can never be. I am a part of you now. You are forever bound to me as I am to you," said Lun within her mind.

Faith cried as Fyreon approached her and cried along with her. The other Titans cried as well. The Existence's tears were so powerful, it conjured a storm over the entire world. "I feel . . . the sorrow of all of the Earth; I think those that are grateful are expressing their sadness as well," said Faith.

The Existence said to her, "Are you ready to go back to Earth?"

"Yes, but I'm not sure where I will go. I am homeless, the world war separated the earth, and . . . I'm terrified," said Faith.

"Do not fear, for I am with you, Moonchild. I shall give you and all those that come after guidance. I shall take a more active role in the future of humanity," said The Existence.

And with that, Faith was brought back to Earth, where she willed a chariot of mana and rode back to her home. She was greeted by an apologetic Johal. The farm was filled with great crops, people of the village rejoiced upon her arrival. After Faith explained what happened, Chief Is'kah thanked her and Lun. The Nephilim had gone into hiding, fearful of the wrath of The Existence and his holy Titans. And so there she lived and protected her village, married, and gave birth to many children, who eventually went their separate ways and began to fill the Earth. These descendants of Faith became known as Moonchildren.

As for the Nephilim, they begged for forgiveness from the Lord, and in the Lord's infinite wisdom, he forgave them. These Nephilim formed different tribes, who became beings of myth and legends—some benevolent and some evil. But overall, humanity turned a blind eye over the beings known as elves, gnomes, fairies, and other creatures of legend. In this time, the Titans continued to rule over their respective elements, stayed within Paradise and very seldom visited Earth. And the Lord continued to watch over Humanity, further building faith amongst his people in his works. However, for all good there is evil, of which Jamaerah and the Forbidden Ones still perpetuate despite their epic loss.

However, this was not the end of the story. The Moonchildren of today still protect humanity from the forces of evil. Lun remained deep within his slumber. When Faith passed, and she went to his side. Lun's spirit still resided within her descendants.

Chapter 16

A teenage girl and her boyfriend playfully chased each other into an abandoned cathedral. "Heh, come on, Cindy! You know we can't be in here! What if the cops catch us?" said the boy.

"Come on, Arnold! Where's your sense of adventure? Besides . . . I'm feeling in the mood," said Cindy in a sing-song sort of way.

"Huh? Well I mean—" said Arnold flabbergasted.

"Tch, typical boy. Always thinking about one thing," said Cindy as she got intimately close to her boyfriend. They proceed to make out, but suddenly two cloaked figures appeared with candles in hand.

The couple immediately stopped kissing and Arnold said, "Whoa! Uh, sorry for trespassing!" The robed people did not respond, and Arnold felt a chill down his spine, and put a hand on Cindy's shoulder, subtly nudging her toward the exist.

"We'll just, uh, leave! No need to call the cops or anything like that," announced Arnold before he whispered to his girlfriend, "Babe, let's get the fuck out here. These two are giving me the creeps." He looked toward the exit and it was now blocked by two other cloaked figures. "W-Whoa! Look, there's no need for things to get so serious," said Arnold as he and Cindy were now surrounded. Cindy began to giggle maliciously. "Cindy?" said Arnold in confusion.

"Another fresh sacrifice for Lord Scar-li-homun . . . Master Nightingale," said Cindy as one of the members gave her a robe to put on.

"Excellent work, Cindy. Lord Scar-li-homun is pleased," said Nightingale as he emerged from the shadows.

Nightingale looked to be a man in his early to mid-thirties, his auburn hair kept in a ponytail. He wore a brown coat, a grey V-neck, with black combat boots, and dark grey cargo pants. He also wore a necklace of two wedding bands: husband and wife. One of his eyes had a scar over it. On one of his eyes glowed an ominous red for a moment before becoming like the other: a light brown eye. In his hand, he held a staff made of blackened, withered wood, yet it would twitch and flex from time to time as if it were still alive. His protégé Cindy came up to him and Hunter kissed her on the forehead, a brimming pride in his eyes.

"So . . . Arnold, my protégé's little boyfriend, what say you and I have a man-to-man conversation?" he said in a mid-range, British accent, significantly contrasting his protege's American accent.

Arnold began to laugh. "Oh, Cindy, you know this guy? Ha-ha, very funny. T-This was a good prank. I bet it took you and uh . . . Mr. um."

"Nightingale. Hunter Nightingale, Jr.," said the man.

Arnold began to back up and meekly replied, "And a pleasure to meet you, Mr. Nightingale. You really got me . . . but it is getting late, I should probably—"

"You're not going anywhere," said Nightingale flatly. "You see, you are important. You are most integral to our great Lord's plan. You are one of the sacrifices needed to usher in the new age, you see," said Nightingale.

"L-Look, I admit it! I . . . I messed around with few other girls while I was dating your daughter or protégé or whatever. I-I'm so sorry, okay? I admit it! Please let me go," sobbed Arnold.

"I knew it," said Cindy to her master. "That's okay. I cheated on you, too. You weren't my first."

Nightingale gave his protege a dagger and she began to walk toward Arnold. He backed up and grabbed a nearby rusty pipe on the floor. He prepared to defend himself, to which Cindy gave a psychotic grin. She performed several flips and swiftly parried the pipe. She stabbed Arnold in his stomach and he coughed up blood. He dropped the pipe and the other cloaked figures joined in; one of them slid the sacrifice table under him as they all chant. "F'te, F'te Scar-li-homun Mez'h" which means "Awaken, Master Scar-li-homun" in an ancient tongue.

They began to gut him open. His ribcage split open and his heart faintly beat. His blood seeped out and his heart finally stopped beating. His blood dripped down into a white space outside of the natural world called the Void via the sacrifice table. Nightingale's eye began to glow as he began to feel himself grow stronger from the sacrifice. Arnold's soul began to leave his body but before he could pass on, Nightingale grabbed hold of it and separated it into two parts: his spirit and his ghost. The spirit dissipated into the afterlife as the shell known as a ghost was left behind. Nightingale bound it to his will. He reassembled Arnold's body with a single touch of his staff, as though he had never been eviscerated. The man then attached the ghost back to its body, causing it to spring back to life. Arnold outwardly looked normal and even sounded like himself, though his eyes did have a glassy glaze to them now.

"Come on, 'lover;' I'll get you some fresh clothes and take you back to your parents," said Cindy. Arnold grunted, "Okay," and was dragged by the arm by Cindy.

A zealot appeared from the shadows, his rank denoted by the design of his robes. He said, "Master Nightingale, I have news to report."

"Then speak," said Nightingale to the zealot.

"Our agents have acquired a powerful relic we should be able to use as a medium for our lord. The Tablet of Gem-Ni-Gog," said the zealot as he brought the ancient tablet forward.

"Excellent! All is going according to plan," said Nightingale with a laugh. "Cindy!" he said. Cindy looked back at him, with Arnold dressed as he was before. "Be back before midnight. You know how I worry," said Nightingale.

Cindy scoffed and said, "Yes Master."

Chapter 17

A young man made his way into what is known as a Space, the area of the soul where things are stored; almost limitless within ghosts. He opened a door and inside was a little girl, about seven or eight years old. She was dressed in a little azure dress with shiny black shoes and a hairclip in her hair. She sobbed as objects within the room such as toys, a lamp, and books moved around in a tornado-like fashion.

"Hey, kid!" yelled the man as he reached out to her with his Yonica.

"Go away! I don't believe you or that mean lady outside!" said the little translucent girl as the items swirled around faster.

"I know you don't want to believe it. I'm sure any child in your situation wouldn't want to believe it. But it's true; your father killed you to appease your stepmother," he said as he kept his hands raised, slowly walking towards her.

"No, no, no. Get away!" she said as he was pushed back by an unrelenting force.

His earpiece chimed in and the voice of a woman said, "Um, Andre ... I don't mean to be rude, but I'M SURROUNDED BY THESE MASSIVE TREE MONSTERS! Whatever you have to do, you better do it now! I don't know how long I can keep them away!" she said.

The ginger woman, about 5'4 in height, held in her hand a pistol; she quickly shot the tree-like being that lumbered towards her. Towering over her, the monster was at least eight feet tall or more. Its eyes glowed and it roared as it continued to move towards the woman. It gathered a chunk of earth and threw it at her, which the woman avoided by rolling out of the way. It prepared to let out a powerful roar and she took this opportunity to chuck a grenade at its mouth, blowing it up from the inside. She shielded her eyes from the splinters raining from the flaming body of the wooden beast. From the smoke, a spirit rose, wailing as it found another tree to infest. As this occurred, a few more spirits came out of the fallen remains of their other bodies and possessed nearby trees.

"Fuck, fuck, fuck," swore the woman.

"I'm almost done talking to her, Ginny. Keep those tree-ants away from the Space," responded Andre.

"All right, Andre, but make it quick! My ammo may not last!" said Ginny as she dodged out of the way of another angry tree beast.

Andre made his way over to the little girl and showed her a photo of her parents: an older middle-aged man and woman in her thirties. And there she was, the little girl with the biggest grin on her face. "Delilah, please stop this before you really hurt someone. You don't want to go down that road. There will be no good place for your soul to go if you keep this up. You could kill someone! I understand you're in pain, but hurting others won't undo what your father did," said Andre as Delilah looked at the photo.

Delilah asked, "You know my name? No, this is a trick. That picture is fake."

"It isn't," said Andre as he gave her the photo. "All I want to do is help you pass on properly," said Andre as he pulled out a newspaper article that looked to be from the 1920s, the paper yellowed with age. Delilah took up the article in her hands and she begins to remember.

The Space warps back to its former state to when Delilah was still alive. She was running around and playing with her toys, with the warmest smile Andre had ever seen. She accidentally bumped into her stepmother, who looked at her with an angry stare. She grabbed the little girl and proceeded to brutally whip and beat her until the little girl sobbed. Delilah's father simply sat there and watched as she beat his daughter. The memory fast forwarded a bit to later that night. Delilah hid behind the railing of the stairs and overheard her parents talking: "I have had it with that little brat of yours!" said Delilah's stepmother.

"She's just a little girl. You cannot fault her for wanting to play around the house," said Delilah's father.

"Must she be such a damn nuisance about it? Why are we even keeping her anyway? I think we should consider how we are expected to survive the winter," said the stepmother.

"You can't possibly mean that. I refuse to!" yelled Delilah's father.

"It's either her or us! Unless you don't love me? What? Am I not as good as your previous wife? It's not my fault she died, you know," said her stepmother. And then he tearfully left the room as her stepmother sighed.

The final memory Delilah had while alive was being awakened by her father, who then grabbed her and shoved her into a bag. "I'm so sorry, Delilah. I'm so sorry," said her father though his tears. He tied up the bag as she struggled within in it.

"Why, Daddy, why?! Please don't hurt me, Daddy! I'm scared!" pleaded Delilah. But no avail, she could barely see anything. It was very dark and the burlap was hard to breathe through. And then her exasperated breath was stopped by a sudden influx of water—he had thrown her into a well.

"I'm so sorry. Good God, what have I done?!" were the last words Delilah had heard. And then everything went black.

Delilah saw her mother, who reached out to greet her. But then the little girl was dragged back to the land of the living. She tried to fight back, but the sheer power of this force caused her being to split into two halves: from spirit to ghost. The spirit went with her mother, while she had plummeted back into the ground, her grave. And she slept for several decades . . . until a red force caused her to awaken. Her mind filled with an unknown anger. Her emotions had spawned specters of fury to her, which then possessed nearby trees and took form. These hideous beasts attacked several mourners near her gravesite. They ran out in fear as Delilah began to cry.

Delilah began to sob, and Andre was now close enough to hug the saddened child. "It's okay. I can help you get back to your mom. But first . . . can you dispel those tree-ants before they kill my friend?" said Andre. With a hiccough and sob, Delilah nods and waved one of her palms. The tree-ants outside the Space turned back into trees, luckily before Ginny was about to be crushed to death by massive wooden palms. She collapsed to the ground with a grunt and thud. Andre and Delilah came out of the Space; he held her hand with his Yonica as she gently floated.

The Space dissipated and Ginny got up off the ground and said, "About damn time."

"I'm sorry, Miss . . ." said Delilah.

"Don't sweat it, kid. I had everything under control on this end," said Ginny.

Andre snorted, "I'm sure you did. Anyways," Andre got on one knee to speak with the ghost child face to face.

"Are you ready?" asked Andre. Delilah nodded but said, "I'm scared. I just want to be with Mommy again."

"It's okay to be scared, but trust me, you're going to be just fine. Just sit still," said Andre.

He put his hand upon her forehead and focused his will. His brown eyes glowed a slight blue and Delilah felt her entire being move. She was suddenly in the same realm she was when she died—her mother and her spirit were there.

"Mommy?" she said.

"Oh Delilah, you have no idea how long I've waited for this moment!" said her mother tearfully as she held her child in her hands. They passed on to the afterlife. Andre smiled as he saw the mother and child walk into the Beyond.

"Makes all the bullshit in this fucked up world worth it sometimes . . ." said Andre.

"Speak for yourself, Leunis," said Ginny as she shook off her pants to get splinters out.

Chapter 18

Ginny sighed and said to Andre, "I'm tired and hurting; when is Nahid going to get here?"

"In a bit. I contacted him just now," said Andre as he leaned against a tree.

"Well, I wish he would get here faster," said Ginny as she removed another splinter from her leg.

"Complaining about it won't get him here any quicker—it just gives me a headache," said Andre. Ginny sighed and they patiently waited for Nahid to bring Andre's car to them. Andre's car slowly came to a brake on the side of the road; a blur of a humanoid figure holding the wheel dissipated.

"About damn time," said Ginny as she got into the passenger seat.

"Watch your tone, human," announced Nahid as he unlocked the door for Andre.

"I kind of agree with her, but thank you, Nahid. Even though you literally didn't have a choice," said Andre.

"I am bound to your car, thanks to your actions," said Nahid with a trace of spite.

"Maybe you shouldn't have been destroying a village in the Middle East. You're lucky no one got killed or I would have outright destroyed you. Consider it your punishment," said Andre as he looked to the side and pulled onto the road, going the maximum speed he could go on the side road. "Three wishes . . . three wishes and freedom shall be mine, and when they are fulfilled, I will—" said Nahid as he obnoxiously slipped through the stations.

"Or you'll what? You're not going anywhere; you're saving me a literal fortune on gas," said Andre.

"So, did you banish the brat?" Nahid said.

"No, we were able to resolve it peacefully," said Ginny.

"Peaceful, she says," replied the djinn.

"Peaceful by our standards," said Andre. "By my count, that's the fifth ghost this week. I wonder what's causing these ghosts to get so aggressive lately?"

Nahid flipped to a news station and a voice chimed in, "More on tonight's report. Morgana Williams, 34, was found murdered outside of her home. Killed in a ritualistic manner consistent with previous murders conducted by an alleged cult called The Fester, who worships a being called The Diseased King Scar-li-ho-mun?"

"That's still a weird name," said Ginny.

Andre asked, "Any news on Status Quo with that? I think there may be some connection between the influx of angry ghosts and these murders."

"We're looking into it with the police, but it seems like suspects in this cult always end up either hanging in their cells or coming down with some severe illness. They often have to be quarantined from everyone else. Other than that, not much to really go on," replied Ginny.

"I see; we'll get to the bottom of this as always. You feel okay though?" asked Andre, noticing her slightly wince.

"Yeah, I'm fine. I just need to rest these weary bones. I'm tired," said Ginny.

"Weary bones? You're twenty-three! Calm down," said Andre.

"Oh, right. You should have the weary bones, old man. The age twenty-four should be considered middle-aged for you considering how you eat," said Ginny.

"Hey, come on now! Frederica's cooking is not THAT bad," said Andre.

"She's a homunculus! An artificial human! What the hell does she know about eating?!" argued Ginny.

"Nonsense, she and Fred scarf down pizzas like they're water when no one is looking."

"That's literally just junk food," said Ginny.

"So? Junk food tastes good," said Andre.

"I suppose this is a bad time to mention that we have arrived at the ginger-haired one's home," interjected Nahid.

"Do you have somewhere to be, o captive one?" said Andre to Nahid.

"I'm surprised a descendant of those kept in chains is so agreeable to keeping another captive," argued Nahid.

"Don't play that card with me. You're a literal whirlwind of chaos. The second I let you go, you go back to your antics of fucking with humanity. You and my ancestors are not the same plight. They were innocent people who were caught up in the greed of rapacious colonists who sought to claim as much as they could," said Andre.

"Um, I think this is my stop," announced Ginny very awkwardly.

"Oh uh . . . right, um yeah . . . no offense though, Ginny. It's not your fault your ancestors may have done those things," said Andre.

"R-Right . . . oh yeah! You're off tomorrow, aren't you? Lucky bastard," said Ginny.

"Jealous?" said Andre.

"A little. I have to write up a report about this mission," said Ginny.

"Ugh, paperwork," said Andre.

"Yeah—maybe you should try writing one of these up sometimes. I'll want a day off sometimes, too, y'know," said Ginny as she got out of her car.

"You and I both know that your workaholic ass doesn't understand the concept of a 'day off.' You'd be bored out of your mind; you're literally the kind of person who likes to work to have fun," said Andre.

"Oh, shut up!" said Ginny. "Take care and goodnight, Leunis. Oh yeah, and no drinking, I'm going to need to bug you about details about what happened in that Space or whatever."

"What do you mean no drinking? You're funny," Andre smiled and said. "Night, Kravitz. See you later."

Andre and Nahid drove off as soon as Ginny got safely into her house, where she immediately plopped onto her sofa.

The next destination for the two was Andre's apartment. It was a nice apartment complex, not the greatest, but also not the worst. Neighbors were friendly—friendlier than the average neighbor. Maybe it was due to Andre being an amputee, but he'd hate to acknowledge pity. Before Andre got out of the car, he swapped out his Yonica for a regular prosthetic arm. It was certainly not as articulate as the Yonica, but with its dull grey color, it helped not arouse too much suspicion. People start asking too many questions when your arm is glowing blue and white. Andre got out of the car and said to Nahid, "Stay, staaaay," talking to him in a very condescending manner while slowly walking back.

"Fuck off, Leunis. I'm not a dog. I understand that I am bound to the parking space. You don't have to patronize me," said Nahid.

"I know, I just like fucking with you. Night," said Andre as he locked his car and walked up the stairs into his apartment. He walked into the door and headed inside, where he was greeted by a cheerful voice.

"Ah, Master! You've returned! How was your mission? Do you have any wounds that need tending?"

It was Frederica, one of two homunculi created by Andre to make things around the house and outside easier for him. Andre had lost his arm when he was sixteen to a skinwalker, a fearsome creature of Native American myth. The other one, Fred, was likely in the Garden, attending to Andre's things in the Astral Plane. He was not much of a conversationalist nor was he capable of expressing emotion.

"No, no. I'm fine. Ginny got the worst of it, but she'll be okay. The mission went well, a ghost kid was successfully passed on. What have you been up to? And did Fred do that thing I asked him to do?" said Andre.

"The usual: cleaning, cooking. I finished two novel drafts today! One romance, the other is sci-fi. I'm sending them off to my editor tomorrow," said Frederica.

"Ooo, another addition to the Celestial Embers series, I hope? I never really cared for romance," said Andre.

"It's a surprise. I promise you'll get one of the first copies once it's published. It has to go through the works first. You know how it goes. As for Fred, he's working on it. He's been on the internet and been digging through the files that Status Quo gave us," said Frederica.

Frederica's left ear twitched a bit; the twins had a tele-pathic link with each other—the usual tell for when they were communicating was that their ears twitched a bit. "Oh, and he's doing some research on the Forbidden One Scar-li-homun," said Frederica. Her ear twitched again.

"I did not cry when Hector died! Sorry, now he's telling me about that one controversial episode of the show Mi Corazon."

"You know what? I'm going to send you the spoilers of that season you missed out on!" said Frederica to Fred. Her ears twitched constantly as she and her brother argued. It was hard to believe that they were composed of the same being yet were so opposite of each other. Andre went to his room to grab his pajamas and went into the bathroom. He took off his prosthetic and closed the door with his hand. He took a shower, fumbling with the soap as he washed himself. He dried off and looked at himself in the mirror: dark skin, curly brown hair, light brown eyes. He brushed his teeth and shaved. After cleaning up a bit, he put his glasses back on, slung the prosthetic over his shoulder, and headed to bed for the night.

"What a day," he thought to himself. "What am I gonna even do on my day off?" He plopped down into bed and put his phone on its charger. He then played with his smartphone for a while before finally drifting off into a slumber.

Chapter 19

The next morning, a well-dressed man who looked to be in about his thirties, drove his nice, expensive car into a parking lot. He wore a white dress shirt and black tie with a blue pea-coat, and an orange paperboy-style hat. He adjusted the rear-view mirror, showing his brownish-maroon eyes. He got out of the car, walked to an agreed-upon spot, and looked at the time on his pocket watch, which was silver plated. He casually leaned against the wall and saw a man with a briefcase come forward. This man was about in his mid-fifties, had blue eyes, and a very poor combover of balding grey hair. He was dressed like he worked in an office space, which he did.

"You're on time. Good," said the suited man in the hat.

"Yeah, yeah, let's cut the BS. Here's your cut of my latest operation. I don't know how you keep orchestrating shit to keep this all under wraps, but I thank you for it," said the office worker.

"Good work, Winston. Lemme check that out," said the suited man. Winston looked around and opened the case; the suited man counted the money to make sure it was all there.

"So, Don, remember when you said you'd claim my soul after twenty years as part of our little arrangement?" said Winston.

"Yup, and I aim to collect when the time comes," said Don as he took the case from him.

"Well, I've decided to change the agreement," said Winston.

"On whose authority?" asked Don.

Winston said, "Well, the actual authorities."

"POLICE! DON'T MOVE!" shouted an officer as he and his partner aimed guns.

Don puts up his hands and said, "You shouldn't have done that."

Don pressed a button on his pocket watch, stopping time before the officers got a shot off. Winston swore and ran off, but Don threw the briefcase at his feet, causing him to fall face first into the cement.

The suited man picked Winston up by the shirt, and said, "I guess I'll just have to collect right now then, you dirty rat."

Winston shakily replied, "Wait, we can work this ou—"

"Fuck that. You lost your chance at negotiation. Now, let's get out of here before this time stop crap runs out," said Don as he willed a portal into existence. He grabbed Winston by the throat and jumped into the portal with him in hand. Winston crashed down onto the ground with a thud and Don released his grip.

They were now in dimly lit room, the walls were dark brown, and the floor was a lighter shade of brown wood. Don picked up Winston with one hand and threw him into a rolling chair.

"W-Where the fuck are we?" asked Winston.

"In Hell, of course," said Donovan.

"H-HELL? Wait . . . does that mean you're actually—?" said Winston in an exasperated tone.

"A demon? Yeah, I'd have no reason to lie about that. But this isn't about me, it's about you right now. Long story short, you belong here now. Congratulations! But it's no fun torturing an old man so . . . 3 . . . 2 . . . 1 . . ." counted off Don. Winston's hairline grew back and his hair lost its salt and pepper color and went back to a shiny brown, his wrinkles dissipated, and he looked about thirty years younger now.

"There we go! Whoa, man, I bet you were a real lady killer in your prime!" said Donovan with a laugh.

He pulled out a mirror and Winston looked at it in shock, feeling his face. He was in disbelief. "How the hell is this possible? I-I, holy fuck. The Existence—please save me!"

"No, no, my friend. You're bound to the land. Here's the deed that proves it," said Don as he pulled out a contract, signed by none other than Winston P. Hughes. Winston tried to take it, but Don kicked him back into the chair. Several demonic figures in suits came through the door.

Don said, "Got a new fresh soul for y'all to have fun with. I got the contract signed and everything. Well, Winston, old boy, I suppose this is where we part ways—nice knowing you! It's like a great man once said, 'For what shall it profit a man, if he shall gain the whole world, and lose his own soul?'"

One of the demons pulled out a long blade, often used for flaying souls in Hell slowly and methodically.

"D-Donovan, wait!" said Winston as he desperately reached out an arm as he was surrounded by the demons.

"Time waits for no man, motherfucker. I gotta go," said Donovan as he was about to summon a portal back out to the Earth. He was stopped by a demon woman, who whispered in his ear. "Huh? The old man wants to talk to me? Is it important?" asked Donovan.

"It sounded pretty important—you probably want to go. It's not wise to upset a Great Duke," said the woman. Donovan rolled his eyes and closed the door, muffling Winston's pained cries and screams.

"Oh, right; can you like file this or whatever for me? I'm garbage with paperwork," said Donovan as he handed the woman Winston's contract.

"No problem!" responded the woman.

After a quick elevator ride up, Donovan walked into an entrance room where there was a secretary that attempted to stop him from entering. Donovan burst through the door and there was the Great Duke, Eligos. He was a large powerful demon, his skin a lavender color, and he sported a large black beard; horns and a crown of fire circled his head. He wore an expensive-looking suit and held in his large palms a phone. He yelled, "Damn it, Aban! I'm on the phone!"

"Well, you summoned me up about something serious—now what it is it? And for the hundredth time, I go by Donovan for right now," said Don.

"I'll call you back. My fool of a grandson is here," said Eligos and he put down the phone. "First of all, how dare you enter my domain without calling first! Second, I don't keep up with all the different aliases you come up with," said Eligos.

"Is there a rest stop between here and the fucking point, old man?" asked Don.

"My damn watch is missing and I know you took it," said Eligos. Don tossed it to his grandfather, which he caught in one hand. "What the hell is all of this silver nonsense? It was bronze before!" said Eligos.

"That ancient thing was rusted to hell. It needed to be re-plated. Besides, I just borrowed it," said Don.

The demon slammed his fist on the desk and said, "Things to be borrowed require permission from the borrowed party!"

"Oh, my bad. Anyways, we done here? I got some other stuff I gotta take care of," said Donovan.

Eligos grumbled, "That was all."

"Oh, and do me a favor? Could you press the button on it in after like a minute? I used it for something," said Donovan before he walks out of the office. The time-frozen cops and the lifeless body of Winston could be seen. Donovan drove out of the parking lot in his nice car. Eligos sighed and pressed the button, resuming time after Donovan escaped.

"That boy is just like his mother," said Eligos with a sigh.

Chapter 20

The usual alarm clock went off on his phone, bringing Andre up like a stiff corpse. He dismissed the alarm with a press of a button and looked at the time, six a.m. He got out of bed and stretched. He felt joints popping and let out a sigh of relief. He put on his stump sock and slid on his drab, grey prosthesis. He walked out his bedroom to greet Fred, who was reading a newspaper, focusing on an article concerning the Scar-li-homun Murders. He put it down for a moment, his usual emotionless expression present on his face, and unamused eyes looked at Andre before saying in a deadpan voice, "Good morning, Master. I hope you are well."

"I am. How are you, Fred? Any breakthroughs with this murder stuff?" responded Andre.

"I am fine. Thank you for asking. To answer your question, I have not found much to go on. I even tried using tracking magic with Frederica to find a source, but to no avail. Whoever is controlling this cult is very clever. But I have hope we will find them," responded Fred.

"I know we will—we always pull through," said Andre as he put a hand on Fred's shoulder and smiled. "You should try smiling sometimes, buddy," he added on.

"You know I am incapable of such an action," replied Fred.

Andre said, "Incapable? Or won't?"

The fire alarm beeped as smoke rose out of the kitchen. "Frederica tried making eggs again?" asked Andre.

Fred nodded in response. Frederica shut off the alarm and put the frying pan into the sink under cool water after throwing out the charred mass of what were once eggs. Andre walked into the kitchen and Frederica looked like a deer caught in headlights, "Ah! Master, I'm sorry. I was trying to make you breakfast and then . . . this happened."

"It's fine; at least you didn't burn down the apartment. I think I'll go to Hunny's this morning," said Andre.

"I understand . . . oh right, you're off today, aren't you?" said Frederica.

"Yup, yup," responded Andre.

"Need me to do anything while you're out and about?" asked the homunculus.

"Work with Fred on finding out more about those murders. Oh, and play nice with Fred, please. You are siblings after all."

Fred retorted, "Well, technically we are the result of our core splitting into halves while still in our clay foundation."

"Ah, yes, my happy little accidents," said Andre with a smile. He grabbed some orange juice and went back to get changed. He ironed with his only hand and held the clothes still with his prosthesis. He walked out in a hoodie, jeans, and sneakers. He ran his fingers through his hair and was good to go.

Andre stepped into the streets and waved hi to some neighborhood kids. They were playing basketball. Maybe someday they would make it to the pros. He looked in the general direction of some teens hanging out. They were chilling but one could clearly see that they were chatting up with a crackhead. The shaky, twitchy young woman slid the young man some cash and he slid her a bag of crack; all one swift motion. Andre frowned and shook his head while walking away. Only two futures in that type of life: death or jail.

He headed to his car and said, "Morning, Nahid."

"Good morning, prison warden. Where are we headed?" said Nahid.

"Hunny's," said Andre.

"Of course, we are . . . very well. Let's go there. The less I see of you, the better," said Nahid.

Andre got to Hunny's diner. It stood in all its old fashioned, beautiful glory. Hunny's was founded after the Civil War by Patricia "Hunny" Phillips and her husband Nathaniel Phillips. It was somewhat of an epicenter of black history and had long since stood the test of time between the Harlem Renaissance, the Civil Rights Movement, and many other events in African American history. Andre was about to go inside and accidentally bumped into a man—about in his thirties—wearing a baseball cap with a hoodie. He had some very distinctive brownish maroon eyes. "My bad, man," apologized Andre.

"All good, kid. Just be more mindful," responded the man. The man opened the door for him, letting Andre go first and then followed him in.

A young waitress greeted them, "Welcome to Hunny's! My, my, my; if it isn't Dre . . . and, oh my gosh, Donovan! Welcome!"

"Hey, Holly!" said Donovan as she gave him a quick hug. "How's your mom?"

"Oh, you know, busy as always. Luckily, the table you always sit at is open!" replied Holly.

"Aw, great!" said Donovan as he went over to his usual table. He had known the Phillips family since Hunny's grandmother, but obviously kept this under wraps by assuming the identity of a family member from a fabricated family name of Clothier.

"Heh, sorry about that, Dre. That's an old family friend. It's like those Clothier men must have a cloning machine or something. They're a dead ringer for their several times great grandpa, I swear to The Existence. Anyways, table for one?" asked Holly.

"Yes ma'am. And the usual, please?" said Andre.

"Cup of coffee, three pancakes, and some scrambled eggs. I'll go give your order to the chef," said Holly as she left him.

"Tell Paul I said hi," said Andre. Andre looked at Donovan for a moment and then took a seat. Donovan called over to another waitress and said, "Hey, Dawn, could I have just a cup of coffee and some pancakes, please?"

"Of course! I'll be right back with a cup of coffee for ya. Can't let our best customer down!" said Dawn as she quickly got him a cup of coffee and put an order in with the cook. Andre got his coffee as well and sipped it.

Donovan took a sip of his coffee. His text alert buzzed and the message said, "You interested in a job?" from an anonymous number.

"Depends, you got my fee?" responded Don.

"Of course. The first half is given upfront, the other half when the job is done," responded the message.

"So . . . we fishing or tanning?" responded Donovan. Those were his code words for "murder" and "espionage." Those were his usual side jobs. Donovan had been a hired gun/sword/what- ever for the last few centuries and he was very, very efficient at his job.

Chapter 21

Andre got his food and thanked Dawn for the speedy service; he checked his phone and got a text from a familiar number: Afenti Marie-Pierre, known affectionately by Andre as Madame. She was a kind old woman from Haiti who had raised him from the time that both of his parents died. She was a powerful mage of voodoo shamanistic background; she trained him in all she knew of magic as well did things for the gods of voodoo known as The Loa.

The text read, "Greetings, Andre. I hope you are well. Just checking in on you to make sure you are alright."

"I'm fine, Madame. How are you?" texted Andre.

"I am well! I am currently in the British Isles, seeking a tome which Ayezan seeks."

"Ah, I see. Seems like the Loa always have their followers doing something," responded Andre.

"It is the Will of the Loa. How is the Yonica doing?" replied Madame.

"Combat-wise, it is perfect. It is a step up from the prototype. It is still not ready for civilian use though," said Andre as he ate another bite of pancake.

"I see. Well, the prosthetic's power is affected by the mental state of the user. You will get there some day. In the meantime, I hope that other false arm is sufficient."

"Hey, just had a quick question for you while we're talking. I'm investigating some murders that may be connected to a cult who worships a Forbidden One. My team and I have had no luck on finding a lead to them. Any suggestions?" asked Andre.

Madame replied, "I would suggest trying to contact an elemental or perhaps the spirits of the victims."

"That's a great idea, Madame. I have to go. TTYL. Love you," said Andre.

"Love you, too. Be safe, my child," responded Madame.

Andre's coffee started to get cold. He whispered the spell, "Calor," heating it up again. He finished his food and paid his bill as well as left a tip. Don sensed the feeling of magic but could not quite pick up who it was coming from. He looked around a bit and thought, "Eh, probably just a fairy getting pancakes. The bastards love those, so long as they aren't causing trouble. I'll leave it alone."

Don eventually finished his meal and left a generous tip. Don got into his car and started it. He adjusted his rearview mirror and saw a familiar face, one which he was startled to see.

"If you're going to just creepily sit in my backseat, you could at least buckle up," said Don.

The angel said, "Not necessary. I am not truly here right now. Would you care to explain how a Winston P. Hughes has been damned to Hell?"

"He made a deal with a devil, of course; greed got to him," explained Don.

"A deal that you had the choice to make," reminded the angel.

"Don't make it out to be solely my fault. He could have said no. He made a choice. Besides, he betrayed me," said Don.

"But you put that man in a constant state of threat," argued the angel.

"Fair enough—still not my fault though. Why do desperate people never read their contracts? It clearly said if he tried anything funny, I get to instantly take him to Hell. Anyways why are you here? Another lecture about how I should repent and devote my life to The Existence again?" said Don.

"A bit more dire than that, my child," said the angel.

"Don't you start with that 'child' stuff. I'm over 700 years old, Israfil," replied Don.

"And I am as old as the Beginning. You are a child to me, Son of Man and the Fallen," said the angel.

"I'd rather you call me child than that. What's the 'dire' thing you need to discuss with me?" asked Don.

"The job you plan to undertake will put you right in the crossfire of a Forbidden One," said Don.

"Ah, one of The Existence's abandoned children," said Don.

"Not abandoned. They abandoned him and refuse to apologize for betraying him," replied the holy being.

"But what's the big deal? It's just a Forbidden One. What will they do? Kill me? I'll just go back to Hell. It's not so bad for demons," said Don.

"You are half human as well—your ultimate fate is uncertain," said the angel.

"All right. So, I'll assume that was the dire thing you wanted to discuss, right? I appreciate the heads up; well, I better get going," said Donovan as he began to drive onto the road and started moving.

"No. There is something else. You will encounter a descendant of Lun," said the angel.

"A Moonchild? So what? I've met with plenty of them before. Most of them are assholes. What of it?" said Donovan.

"This one is the descendant of Thaddeus Leunis," said the angel.

Donovan immediately drove his car to a nearby parking area and turned off the car and said, "No. No fucking way. You're bullshitting me. Thad's family died in that car accident over a decade ago. You have a lot of fucking nerve—"

"Hold your tongue, Aban. Archangels do not lie. You know this to be true," said the angel.

"No. How is this possible? I looked and searched and I . . ." said Don while shaking his head in denial.

"The Existence has plans for the descendant of Thaddeus," said the angel.

"What kind of plans?" asked Don.

"That I do not know. The Lord's motives and plans are unknowable even to me," said the angel.

Don sighed, "Fuck! What if I don't take this job?"

"It matters not what you do; it will happen regardless of your choice. The Lord has willed it so."

"Fuck the Lord!" said Don as he turned around.

Israfil was gone.

"Be careful, Aban," echoed the voice of Israfil. Don sighed and thought to himself before saying, "Fuck. I don't need this right now. Thad, if you're up there, and this is true, I will keep my promise. I swear it," said Don.

Chapter 22

Andre drove to his local magic shop, where many things of the arcane arts existed. Fred had called ahead for Andre and requested a book called *Invertum Respirum* Vol. XIII. Andre walked up to the shopkeeper. "What's up, Hank?"

Hank replied, "Good morning, Mr. Leunis. Frederick called. I know the book you seek. Here it is." He rang Andre up and Andre slightly winced at the price.

I should be sending the bill to Status Quo for this. The things I do for this damn job, thought Andre to himself. He received the book in a bag and wished Hank a good day.

Andre walked out of the shop and thought to himself, *I'm not even supposed to be working right now, yet here I am.* Andre set the book on the passenger's seat and drove to the park and decided to go for a walk.

The park was a large beautiful area that was kept up by the city—with lush green grass and tall old trees. The park was lively and there were humans all about. A family could be seen at a picnic; there were joggers and even pixies moving around disguised as fireflies. Andre sensed their energy, and one of them annoyingly tried to fly around him, leading to Andre swatting it away.

The pixie revealed its true self in a veiled form and said, "That hurt, meanie!"

"Well, maybe you shouldn't buzz around people's faces so damned much," said Andre.

The pixie stuck out its tongue before disappearing as a sprite once again.

"Hello? Can anyone hear or see me? Hello? HELLOO! I REALLY NEED SOME HELP HERE!" said a voice behind Andre. Andre turned around to see the ghost of a man floating around a bunch of people. Most people could not see spirits—only certain individuals could. Andre decided to approach. Maybe this poor ghost just needed some help.

Andre whispered a spell, "Humilis Disputatio." "Low talk" in Latin. This allowed him to speak so only individuals he picked could hear him.

"Hey, buddy! Over here!" said Andre to the spirit, who looked right at him.

"Ah! You, you can see me? Thank the Lord!" said the ghost of a man as he floated over to Andre. The man was a translucent version of his original self.

"Oh shit, you're Christopher Harris!" said Andre, recognizing the man after adjusting his glasses.

"Wait, how did you know my name?" asked Mr. Harris.

"It's a long story. I know you have a lot of questions right now and I'm more than happy to explain them, but uh, maybe we should go somewhere more private," said Andre.

He saw people talking to each other, wondering why he was talking to himself. Harris nodded and followed Andre to a less-crowded place.

Andre made a quick trip to his car and pulled out a file and showed Harris his picture. "So, first, we need to get this out of the way. I'm sorry to be the one to tell you this but, Mr. Harris, you are dead," said Andre.

"W-What? But that's not possible! I'm standing right here talking to you. Well, floating, but that doesn't make any sense!" said Harris.

Andre sighed and replied, "I wish it wasn't true, but it is. You were one of the victims of what is known as the Scar-li-ho-mun Murders. You were actually murdered in this park." Andre showed him pictures on his phone of the murder scene. Harris's throat was slit, ritualistic carvings and cuts, and he was sprawled out on the floor.

"No . . . no . . . my wife, Karen, is she—?" asked Harris.

"Your wife and kids are safe, but they miss you dearly," said Andre.

"No . . . no!" said Harris in denial as he teared up.

"I know, this situation is horrible. I'm sorry you and your family have to go through this. And I know your spirit is suffering.

The fact that your ghost is here speaks volumes. You haven't passed on completely," said Andre.

"What do you mean? Aren't a ghost and a spirit the same thing?" asked Harris.

"Contrary to popular belief, they are not. Beings are comprised of two things: a body and a soul," explained Andre. "The body is simply a shell for the soul. And beyond that, the soul itself is a volatile force that can manifest in different ways. When a person dies, the main essence, the spirit, passes on to the afterlife. However, the thing known as emotion can cause a spirit to leave an imprint of some sort in the mortal plane. In your case, you are a ghost. You are literally the embodiment of your memories."

"Wait, so I'm not even me?" said Harris.

"Well, yes and no. You're here for a reason. My associates and I think it may tie into the murder. Lately, a lot of ghosts have been waking up and I've had to banish a few and help the others pass on. And in between that, I've been talking with them to learn as much as I can to prevent more killings. Do you remember anything before you died?" said Andre.

"I don't, sadly. I just remember going for a run and the next thing I know I'm floating around the park for the next few days," replied Harris.

"I see. Well, I think I may have a way to help you. But I must warn you, it may bring up some scary memories. Are you okay with that?" said Andre.

"If this will prevent more people from being murdered, then I'd be more than happy to help. Do what you have to," said Harris.

"Wonderful, and once we're done here then I'll see if I can help you pass on," said Andre.

"Wait, before you do that, can you pass on a message for me to my wife and kids? Just tell them that I love them very much?" asked Harris.

"Of course. I promise I will. Are you ready?" asked Andre as the fingertips of his hand glowed blue. Harris nodded.

"This won't hurt a bit, physically anyway," said Andre as he plunged his hand into Harris's being.

In a hazy replay of events, Harris and Andre saw his memories up until when he was murdered. Harris kissed his wife, all dressed up in his usual running gear. They lived near the park. He got to a point where he ran an underpass in the park and was tackled by a man wearing a hoodie. Harris tried to wrestle the man off of him but he was gripped by the man with an overwhelming, almost otherworldly strength. The figure's hood was knocked off and the young fellow was a teenager with the look of a serial killer.

"A revenant!" said Andre.

The teenager chanted, "Scar-li-ho-mun" and brutally stabbed Harris in the chest. The revenant pulled out Harris's heart and put it into a sack while running off. The next moment Harris's spirit floated up to pass on and an angel's arm was outstretched to catch him, but there was a sharp pain as a hook stabbed into Harris's soul's side. It ripped out his ghost and the spirit was pulled into Paradise.

A voice echoed, "Your ghost shall serve me. Your time is not yet done. You will be fodder for the Diseased King."

But Harris's ghost was able to rip himself away from the hook and screamed for help.

Harris and Andre were immediately drawn back to reality and they both started panting.

"Holy fuck, what was that thing that killed me?" yelled Harris.

"A revenant. Body and ghost pulled into one to produce one scary, powerful creature that serves a master. He looks young .. . fuck, I don't recognize him from the case files. The Mastermind must be using revenants to conduct the murders . . ." said Andre.

"But more to that, what did that guy mean by 'fodder'?" asked Harris.

"Certain magi have the ability to draw upon a ghost's essence and use it to amplify their power." *What do the Forbidden Ones have planned?* said Andre to himself.

"Wait, does that mean I won't have an afterlife if I get absorbed by that Forbidden thing?" said Harris while hyperventilating.

"It's okay, Mr. Harris. I won't let that happen. Let's see what we can do about getting you passed on. This has been very fruitful for me! Thank you!" said Andre.

Harris nodded, but was clearly confused about this whole situation.

Andre closed his eyes and focused. His hand glowed with a blue energy once again and raised his palm to the ghost, but there was no effect. "Huh? What the hell? That usually works!" said Andre with surprise.

"I . . . I felt a warm light, but I was immediately dragged back here, almost like I was chained somehow," responded Harris.

"Hold on, I'll be right back," said Andre as he headed to his car once again. He came back with a piece of sage and began an incantation to help spirits pass on. He held the sage up and blue energy flowed through it, producing an aquamarine aura, and he gently waved it over Harris. Harris struggled and fell flat to the ground.

He tried to fight the feeling. "Damn it!"

"You said it. Looks like the Mastermind has found a way to bind you here. The only thing I can do now is to keep you safeguarded. I'll be right back, stay right where you are," said Andre as he went back to his car. He came back with an old school camera.

"What is that?" asked Harris.

"It's a camera," said Andre.

"I figured that, but how will that safeguard me?" asked Harris.

Andre tested the camera by snapping a photo and the camera quickly produced a quick image, which he pulled out and shook. "Have you ever heard locals of Third World countries talk about the superstition of taking their photos? They believe it will take their soul. Well, there's a half truth to that. This old-school type of camera is capable of sealing ghosts into photographs. While you are in the photograph, it should make you more compact and easier to protect from danger. Understand?" said Andre as he pointed the camera toward him.

"I don't understand all of this, but you're the first person I've been able to talk to in a while. So, do what you think you must. And thank you for your help," said Harris.

Andre snapped his photograph, drawing the ghost into the camera to where he was put into a photograph. He shook it out and Harris's voice immediately said, "Whoa, whoa! Careful I'm getting dizzy!"

"Sorry," said Andre as he looked at Harris in the frame.

"This feels kind of calming in a way," said Harris as he moved in the photograph.

"I hear that a lot when I bind spirits like this. So, what I'm going to do for now is bring you to my place to be guarded by a couple of associates of mine," said Andre as he stored the photo of Harris away and went back to his car. *Always working even when I'm not working,* thought Andre to himself.

Chapter 23

Andre drove back home with Harris in hand and saw Frederica making some edits to her manuscript with a pen.

"Oh hi, Master! Back so soon?" said the homunculi.

Andre showed her the picture of Harris.

"Oh, wow, I thought you weren't supposed to be working today," said Frederica.

"Yeah. Me too. Anyways, this is Christopher Harris. He's the ghost of one of the murder victims. I need you to do me a favor and look after him for a bit."

"Uh, hello?" said Harris as he looked at the young lady.

"You got it, Master! I will do my very best for you! So, Harris, how do you feel about romance novels?" asked Frederica to the ghost as she gently laid him down on the couch next to her and kept writing.

I thought your suffering was supposed to end after you died, thought Harris. "Thank you, ma'am. Anyways, I'm going to hit up a club," said Andre as he went to his room.

"Oh okay! You have fun!" said Frederica to Andre.

Andre once again ironed an outfit one-handed and put on his ensemble of a suit coat, a red dress shirt, black slacks, and some black shoes. He strapped on his prosthetic arm again and combed his hair. He put on some shades and waved farewell to Frederica as he drove out. He intended to go to his usual spot; the sun was setting down. It was almost six p.m.

"You look absurd," said Nahid.

"Oh, fuck off, you know I look good. You're just hating as usual," said Andre as he parked his djinn-bound car in the parking lot. Nahid sighed. Andre waited in line and greeted the bouncer before heading in. The bass was pounding outside the door; the lights and a fog machine were going. The room was a hazy purple and there was a second story.

A familiar face greeted him. "Ay, what's up, Dre?"

Andre gripped the man's hand and gave a quick hug with the prosthesis. "Not much, Mike! How are you?" said Dre.

"Bro, it's fuckin' bumpin' in here tonight. You're right on time. I'm surprised you were able to get away from that desk of yours. You never get that!" said Mike as he wrapped his arms around two girls.

"You know how it is, gotta work hard before you can play hard," said Andre.

"True, true. All right, man, I'll get at you later," said Mike as he walked away.

Andre approached the bar and saw his familiar bartender, Martin. "Martin! How's it going?" asked Andre.

"Going great, Dre. Didn't expect see your sorry ass back here," said Martin teasingly.

Andre scoffed and said, "Good one, man. We need more assholes like you in the world."

They both shared a good laugh. Martin chimed in, "Oh yeah! I got something new in club's latest shipment! Check it out."

He showed Andre a bottle of some fancy rum and Andre said, "Oh, fuck yeah! Let's rip right into this bad boy! Let me get some coke! As a matter of fact, let me get this whole bottle!" said Andre as he slapped down some cash. He got some Coke, poured it in along with the rum and proceeded to drink one.

"Whew, that's good and strong. Just how I like it. It's called Seafarer? That's a neat-ass name," said Andre as he examined the bottle. An old sailor in a navy-blue outfit was on the bottle.

"Take it easy, Leunis. I don't want to have to babysit you like last time," said Martin.

"Yeah, yeah," said Andre as he got a text message on his phone. It was from Ginny and read: "I know you're probably out right now, but please don't get super-duper hammered. I need you to be at your best."

"Yeah, yeah. I hear you loud and clear," said Andre.

"You got it, Kravitz." She sent a smiling emoji back.

"I swear that woman has like a sixth sense or something," said Andre to Martin.

"Yeah, I bet," said Martin as he tended to some other customers.

Andre thought to himself, *I'm bored. Time to be nosy.* He focused his mind and slowly began to see the Sensations of the club. A Sensation was the aura a feeling gives off, usually in the form of a color along with a taste or smell of sort to it. This ability was privy only to Moonchildren, due to it being the one of the Titan Lun's Responsibilities: Empathy. As useful as this ability may seem, it was very stressful due to always knowing what those around a Moonchild felt, and sometimes negative energy would rub off them. Andre learned from Madame a method to put up "Walls" within his mind to prevent Sensations from seeping in without his permission.

Andre slowly undid the Walls of his mind; he was now open to the minds of the club. He often did this to sense the general vibe of the club. He sensed several emotions: anger, sadness, boredom, and a mix of happiness motivated by drunkenness. His sight extended to the scene of two men punching each other, a reddish aura engulfing them both as they struck each other with a flurry of fists.

I'm guessing someone's lady hasn't been all that faithful. Or just typical alpha male shit, thought Andre. His attention turned to the sight of a beautiful young woman, a sad aura surrounding her. "Aw, poor gal. I hope what it is, she overcomes it. Depression's a motherfucker," he said as he took another shot.

Andre proceeded to chug the whole bottle as Mike noticed, "Holy shit, man! You are killing that!"

Nearby patrons start to yell, "Chug! Chug! Chug!" He slammed the bottle down, having downed all of it. Andre went out to the dance floor and started dancing with several women. He could sense the aura of happiness and a hint of lust in the room. The rest of the night was a blurry haze for him.

Chapter 24

The next morning, Andre awoke from his drunken haze and was in an unfamiliar room. He was naked and noticed condoms. *At least I wasn't drunk enough to forget protection,* thought Andre. He assessed his surroundings more, clothes hastily thrown about, his prosthetic was on the floor, his glasses were on the nightstand, and a naked woman lay next him. She was gently sleeping. She was tanned skinned, brown haired, and very pretty. He checked his phone and saw that there were several missed calls and texts from Ginny. He looked at the time. It was four a.m.

"Oh shit!" He looked at the texts. "Boss is coming in for inspection. Need you here ASAP."

"This is super important."

"Damn it, Andre. Please get here. NOW. I need help."

Andre sighed and got dressed, sliding on his clothes before putting on the prosthetic, and he heard the woman stir a bit. She said with a drowsy, faint smile, "Heading out so early?"

"Yeah, I have to help a friend with something. It's not that I haven't enjoyed our night together. Well, what I remember of it, but this is an emergency . . . um . . . Mandy?" responded Andre.

"Mindy," she corrected him as she could barely stay awake.

"Mindy, Mindy . . . right! Uh, gotta go!" said Andre as he quickly headed out, but not before flushing down any used condoms he may have left. He couldn't have any other little Moonchildren running around. Moonchildren were notorious for wreaking havoc and destruction if they weren't trained or taught what their purpose was.

After calling Nahid to pick him up and playground-worthy round of insults and spiteful comments, he got to his apartment. Frederica asked him if he was all right but sensed the remnant lust aura on him and simply sat back down. She simply went back to working on her manuscript as Harris contemplated whether if agreeing to staying here was a good idea or not. After a speedy shower and a quick change of wardrobe into something more professional, Andre broke several traffic laws by making Nahid cloak and float the car over most of the traffic. After a hurried run inside Ginny's office, Ginny and Bill Harvey, their boss, were talking.

"Ah. It's so good of you to turn up, Mr. Leunis. That's another infraction, late employee," said Harvey as he made another note on his clipboard. Ginny had a nervous look on her face as she looked at Andre with pleading eyes.

"I-I'm sure Andre has logical reason as to why he was late," said Ginny. Ginny looked at Andre and Andre produced the photograph of Harris.

"A picture of one of the murder victims?" asked Harvey.

"Wrong. What I hold in my hand is the ghost is one of the victims. Christopher Harris," said Andre.

Harris awkwardly said, "I mean it is true. He saved me from aimlessly floating around with no one to hear me."

"Ah, I see. Any new leads based upon information from Mr. Harris?" said Harvey, unfazed. He had seen so many supernatural entities over the years. And he had killed many of such entities.

"We've learned that they're using revenants to commit murders as well as have been using ghost's residual spirit energy to power up something. I hypothesize that they plan to summon Scar-li-homun using said energy," said Leunis.

"Interesting theory, have you found his stronghold yet?" asked Harvey.

"Nothing yet," said Leunis. Harvey walked up to Andre, whom he barely looked up to.

"Then you better find out quick. People are dying. I hope you two realize that. And another thing. This Mickey Mouse way you have of running this sector is garbage," said Harvey.

"Bullshit. Look at our mission success rates. And you're one to talk. Sitting over in the great government halls while us peons die and then fade away like we were never important," said Andre.

"What was that, Leunis? Don't you compare me to Senate Joe and Representative Sam up there. You know who keeps this operation going? You know who keep the lights going in this place? People like me. A normal fucking human being. Not Werewolf Slayer Raggedy Ann and The One-Armed Wonder. Without assholes like me, the world would become a lot less unprotected. A scary place. A dog-eat-dog world. There's an order to things, Leunis. And you don't seem to get that, just like your father, who was a vigilante who took the order of things and bent it to only benefit him. And then he died for it," said Bill.

Andre clenched his fist in anger. He was a hair away from punching his Boss. But Bill knew better. Andre knew better. He let it go and simply nodded. Bill looked around and said, "You're on a deadline, people. Get the job done." Bill put on his fedora. "Or I'll find some people that fucking will." He closed the door.

"That fucking dick," said Andre. "What does he think we're doing? We're putting all our effort into finding this fucker!"

"Yeah, also what the hell were you thinking last night? I told you about the drinking!" said Ginny.

"Yeah, yeah, I'm sorry. Really, I mean that," said Andre.

Ginny sighed. "Whatever. Bill left an assignment for us to do. Sit down and I'll give you the details of it."

Andre sat down in one of the nice, swivel chairs that Ginny had in her office. She was mainly the one who handled their Status Quo operations regarding paperwork and other bureaucracy things. Andre hated dealing with that crap. He'd rather just do field-operation things. She adjusted her glasses and opened the file. "Fuck! Three more murders!"

"Whoa, really? At once? Jesus," said Andre as they looked over the case file together.

Chapter 25

The contents of the file were spread out all throughout Ginny's desk. Three victims, all male, of African American descent. Each of them had charges on their records related to drug trafficking and assault. It appeared to have been murder-suicide. One of them killed the other two with a pistol and then proceeded to shoot himself in the head.

"Damn, this looks pretty brutal," said Ginny. "But I don't see how this relates to the Scar-li-homun murders."

Andre noticed a bag of a grey substance. He sensed the residual spirit energy in it. "I think I may have found our link. Ectoplasm. Yuck," said Andre as he felt the contents. It had a cold sensation to it and appeared to lightly twitch in response to his touch.

"Are you gonna do that thing?" said Ginny with a look of disgust.

"I'm going to have to if we're going to prevent more deaths," said Andre as he opened the bag.

He gagged in disgust the second he undid the seal; the smell of ectoplasm was not very pleasant. He put on a glove out of the box that Ginny kept on one of her shelves, dipped a finger in, and put a tiny dot of it on his mouth. Bitter and vile taste aside, he was now in tune with the spiritual energy, which he used to tap into the perspective of the ghost. He immediately sensed what it was—the hatred. The malice this creature had. This was not a ghost's energy; it was a wraith's. A wraith was a creature comprised of a ghost and a specter's energy. A specter was created from residual emotional energy, giving it a form. When a person died with regret and powerful emotional energy, then the specter and the ghost were created. The two entities may fuse together to create an angry, powerful spirit called a wraith.

Andre looked through the eyes of the wraith, seeing a man taking a piss in the bathroom; the wraith was staring at him through a vent. "What a nice first sight," said Andre sarcastically. The man finished up and the wraith phased through the vent and entered the man. Andre could temporarily see the man's spirit, but he was overtaken by the wraith's aura. The man was now possessed. The wraith was in the driver's seat. He zipped his pants and the man looked in the mirror. He was wearing some gang colors as well as a tattoo: a purple and gold theme.

He walked out of the bathroom and saw his homies, who were playing a fighting video game. "Yo Tucker, you want a turn?" said one of the men.

"Oh, what's wrong, Kurt? Tired of getting your ass whooped?" chuckled the other guy on the couch.

"Man, fuck you, Shawn," said Kurt. They both laughed as Tucker's vision turned to a gun on the table along with several bags of dope. Tucker grabbed the gun and shot Shawn first, which caused Kurt to scream.

Kurt tried to pull out his own gun and said, "Whoa, Tucker, the fuck—"

BLAM!

His brains were blown out. Tucker then shakily tried to resist the gun being turned on himself—but to no avail. BLAM!

The shock of it all snapped Andre back to where he was now. "Whoa, shit!" He hyperventilated a bit and Ginny held his shoulder.

"Whoa! Are you okay? Stay with me, Leunis! I need you," said Ginny.

Andre calmed down and said, "Yeah, I'm good now. Damn spiritual feedback. So, we're dealing with a wraith."

"Oh great. Where is it?"

"In the complex still, from the looks of it. I'm guessing it plans to kill more members. From what I got, it may have something planned tonight. We need to move quickly" said Andre.

Ginny gave him a stick of gum to get rid of the taste of ectoplasm but before he put it in his mouth, he dropped to the ground in pain.

He swore and took off his prosthesis. He held on to his vestigial arm and screamed in pain.

"Jesus! Are you okay?" said Ginny as she assisted him to a chair.

"Phantom pain," said Andre in a choked tone.

"Don't push yourself. Breathe," said Ginny as she walked over to her cooler and got him some water.

Andre drank it and his breathing stabilized. He focused his mind and thought to himself. He envisioned his soul as a blue copy of himself. The arm he lost was still connected to his soul and chants, "It's not there" as a mantra. The arm came back under his control and he flexed the spirit of his arm. His stump slightly twitched. He opened his eyes and said, "I'm good. I hate it when that happens."

Ginny said with a concerned tone, "You know, if you don't think you can to do this mission, I can call in some backup to—"

"No, fuck that," said Andre as he put his prosthetic back on. "I got this. No need to call another sector."

"But when that happens, it's good for you to—" said Ginny.

"I said no. I'm a Moonchild, dammit. This shit, spiritual shit, that's my deal. And the fact that this wraith bastard thinks it has the right to take life away just made this personal," said Andre with frustration.

Ginny nodded and said, "Okay, so how about I hang back and coordinate the fire department? If you need any help, then you contact me. I'll be in close vicinity."

"So, we are doing a false fire alarm? That'll piss off the tenants, I'm sure," said Andre.

"Yeah, but there's not much else we can do. We must safeguard human life first and foremost. That's literally Status Quo's motto: Safeguard human life and protect it from the dangers of the supernatural," said Ginny.

Andre snickered and said, "Yeah, I know, Werewolf Slayer Girl."

"Um, hello?" said Harris.

"Oh right, this guy. Sorry, Mr. Harris. I think it's best if you stay with Ginny for now so we can help you," said Andre.

"I really just want to see my wife and kids again," said Harris as he sobbed.

"It's okay, we'll help you. We promise," said Ginny as she consoled him.

Chapter 26

"DING! DING! DING!" sounded the fire alarm. Fire trucks surrounded the complex. The firefighters furiously pounded on the doors of the residents as smoke filled up the building. The occupants rushed out of their apartments, their children, their pets, and whatever valuables they could put fit in their arms. Evacuated by the on-site firefighters, the residents clambered down the steps. Soon enough, the building was cleared. The fire workers pretended to deal with the fire, which was a small controlled fire. Behind the building, Andre begrudgingly put up his handicapped sign for his car. "On the bright side, you get your gloves half off," said Nahid mockingly.

"Fuck you, you're not allowed to laugh at my struggle," said Andre. Nahid continued to laugh and Andre grumbled. He popped open the trunk of his car.

In the truck, there was a large black briefcase. He wore a black hoodie, with his usual chest plate underneath, orange charms hanging on the abdominal part of it to ward off oncoming forces like bullets. He had on grey khaki pants and black combat boots; he chose to put on contacts today rather than his usual glasses. He opened his briefcase and pulled out the Yonica. It was white and blue, the fingers twitched as soon as Andre touched it, and it resonated with his power. He took off his usual prosthesis and attached the Yonica and locked it into place. He moved his fingers in an articulate manner. *I wish I could wear this thing all the time—it would make my life so much easier,* thought Andre to himself. The runic symbols on the fingers glowed from energy provided through the blue core on the palm. Andre pulled out a small collapsible golden staff with similar runic symbols on it. He extended it by three sections, and it locked into place.

Ginny chimed in on her radio, "You ready, Leunis? Over."

"Yeah, just about. Over." He basked in the moonlight for a moment and donned his full-face mask; his eyes glowed a pale blue. He closed the trunk, put up his hood, and walked inside the building.

Andre uttered the word "Noctus" while focusing his will. The world around him shifted; he was now in the Noctus Zone, the area the normal human eye cannot see. Supernatural creatures and spirits often resided in this Zone, the usual tell being the hazy, grey effect around the area. It was not bound to the normal laws of reality, one of which being earthly confinement of objects. As such the area was open beyond the true confines of the complex. He deftly flipped and dodged out of the way of a wild specter. It let out a mighty roar and was bull-shaped.

The specter puffed air out its nostrils. Andre vaulted up in the air using his staff and cracked the beastly specter on the head, which brought it down in a single swoop. "The specter of a bull? How the hell . . ." said Andre. He was hit in the chest by a stray bullet, which knocked him back a bit. His chest plate had protected him. Three ghosts of humanoid shape floated in front of him, holding hazy apparitions of guns. Andre focused his attention on these ghosts.

They fired more bullets and Andre used his Yonica to swat them aside; spirit bullets only had as much power as those who believe in it. Andre called out to them, "Hey hold up! I'm not your enemy!" They are the guys who have been killed! He called out names of these victims: "Kurt! Shawn! Tucker!"

"Yo, hold up. How do you know our names?" asked Tucker, putting down his gun.

"What the fuck happened to us?" asked Kurt.

"I know this is a lot to take in, but . . . y'all are dead," said Andre.

"No fucking way—then how are we talking right now? We should be up in Paradise or whatever," said Shawn.

"Well . . . yes? Maybe? I don't know where people end up— the point is you are ghosts. Not your spirit," said Andre.

Shawn asked, "What's the difference?"

"Huge difference," said Andre as he explained the concept of a ghost and spirit to them. Their guns dissipated, and they simply thought for a moment.

"So . . . let us get this straight . . ." said Shawn.

Tucker said, "Part of us are in the afterlife, but we're like memories in a shell left on this Earth?"

"And you're saying this is all a wraith or some shit's fault? I think this nigga's full of shit. We should dust his ass," said Kurt. The ghosts summoned their guns again.

Andre sighed and launched a ball of spiritual energy at them. It exploded into a massive flurry of blue sparks, filling their being up with holes. "How are we still alive?" said Shawn, who noticed his hands were full of non-bleeding holes.

"I guess we really are dead," said Tucker.

"Now you get it. Look, I'm trying to catch the thing that did this to you guys. It's around here somewhere and I could really use a hand if you are willing to help. I have a way to help you guys pass on regardless though. What do you say, fellas?" said Andre.

The holes in their bodies slowly filled back up and Kurt said, "Aight, I guess."

"What are we up against exactly?" asked Shawn.

"So . . . a wraith is basically a really angry ghost mixed with a specter. The best way to get rid of them is with overwhelming spiritual energy. Hence, why you guys would help make my job easier," said Andre.

"Alright, man. We'll roll with you. Let's get this motherfucker before he bodies more people," said Tucker.

The Ghost Gang and Andre headed deeper into the Noctus Zone. Its massive, hazy-grey void-like structure were filled with doors. They had several other skirmishes with other animal-like specters, more than likely left behind by household pets. "What do you all remember of your lives?" asked Andre as he opened another random door.

"Same old story. Grew up on the rough side of town, sold dope to take care of our families, hard to leave that life," said Tucker.

"My mom used to tell me this life would lead to only two futures: dead or in jail. Guess I should have listened to her," said Shawn.

"If I could take it all back, I would. At the very least try to push Little Tommy away from this shit," said Kurt.

Andre frowned; ghosts were often filled with the regrets of a person after they die. "Who is Little Tommy?" asked Andre.

"A kid who joined up with our crew. Young squirt, about fifteen. Momma and Daddy gone. He only had his grandparents to look after him. His grandpa recently died; he hated us hanging around him—felt that we were corrupting him to a life of crime," said Kurt.

"The boy only had us and his grandma . . ." said Shawn. They all sighed.

"Well . . . maybe I could talk to Little Tommy on your behalf," said Andre.

"We'd appreciate that, man. Thank you," said Kurt.

Andre's newfound information finally clicked. "Oh shit! I think I think know who the wraith is!" said Andre, "What was Tommy's grandfather's name?"

"Uh . . . Mr. Robinson I think?" said Tucker.

"I think when Mr. Robinson died, it created a wraith, one that was aiming at you guys because of Mr. Robinson's regrets and anger!" pieced together Andre.

"Ain't that some shit," said Kurt.

A hooded humanoid with a tattered black cloak rushed out of the next-door Andre opened! It slashed at Andre with long black claws, which Andre narrowly blocked with his staff. Andre willed a series of mana tethers from the Yonica's finger tips and yanked it, causing a wall to crash down onto the creature's cloak. The creature let out an inhuman roar. "I got you now, you damned wraith!" said Andre.

Chapter 27

The wraith screamed, "Even in death, you clowns seek to corrupt my grandson!"

"That was never out intention, Mr. Robinson!" cried Tucker.

"We never meant to involve him in the streets!" said Kurt.

"We're sorry! Honest!" said Shawn. The wraith's eyes glowed red and it pulled back the hood, revealing his face. He was an older man, about mid-sixties, salt and pepper hair, his red eyes filled with fury. His face then contorted into a deformed, pale and ghastly form with an outstretched mouth. It snarled and attempted to swat away the Ghost Gang.

"Ghost Gang assemble!" yelled Andre as he lifted up his staff in the air; it glowed with a golden aura. Tucker, Shawn, and Kurt surrounded him and Andre commanded, "Take the form I command!" Andre stabbed his staff into the ground and the Ghost Gang's forms squashed and stretched until they took the forms of armored knights with lances.

"Whoa, this is cool as hell!" said Kurt. "The ectoplasm ghosts and the like are very versatile and take many shapes. Y'all didn't think you had to stick with the forms y'all died in, did you? Because I know Mr. Robinson sure as hell didn't look like that when he did. Now engage shields!" yelled Andre.

The knighted ghosts brought into existence shields and blocked the oncoming purple fire that the wraith spewed from its mouth. Andre sent the next command to them telepathically and Kurt took a knee, as did Tucker. They interlocked their arms and Andre willed Shawn over to him and molded him into a medium-sized ball. While holding Shawn in one arm, Andre hopped onto Kurt and Tucker's interlocked arms, and with all their might, they flung them into the air. Andre tossed up the ball and whacked it with his staff like a baseball bat. He aimed directly at the wraith's chest, and at the last minute, Shawn took his knightly shape once again and stabbed the creature right in the chest. Shawn rolled out of the way, leaving his lance impaled through the creature. Andre soared through the air and proceeded to whack the wraith in the head with his staff.

He yells the spell, "Electricae!" and lightning crackled from the Yonica to the staff, electrifying the wraith. While the wraith was stunned by overwhelming force, Shawn ripped out his lance, unveiling a ray of light that came out of the wraith's chest. Andre plunged his Yonica inside the creature; he felt the hateful aura of the creature crawl over the arm. Andre used his staff to spit blue flame at him to distract the wraith further. Andre dug deep and ripped out an orb from the wraith.

The shell of the wraith began to hollow and dissipate. Mr. Robinson's voice could be heard saying, "No! No! Tommy—"

"Tommy will be fine. I will take of him and Mrs. Robinson. I promise. But you are going to have to pay for what you did to these men," said Andre as he points toward the ghosts.

"I just . . . didn't want him on the streets," said Mr. Robinson.

"Yeah, but you did that in the wrong way. And now you have to pay," said Andre.

"NEVER," yelled the core as it levitated out of Andre's grip and formed the wraith once more. The wraith lunged at Andre! But it is dragged back by a chain that came from an open door near the wraith. The inside of the door was covered black hell-fire. The wraith was yanked back until it was close enough to the door to be stabbed by a long blade.

The wraith let out a bellowing roar as it finally exploded in a violent cloud of black smoke. A man walked out of the cloud, holding the wraith's core. He was well dressed, a black biker's coat with a mask on; the blade he wielded was a silver great sword that glowed in the moonlight. "I couldn't agree with you more, kid," said the man as the core vanished in flames when he closed his hand.

Andre adjusted his mask in shock. "What the hell!" He sensed a dark energy around the man . . . the malevolent aura of a demon.

"Tch, we can take this motherfucker," said Kurt. Several specters surrounded the man, but he simply summoned chains that dragged the beasts down to Hell.

"Oh look! We're fading!" said Kurt.

"I guess we are passing on now; you got this, right, man?" said Shawn.

"I really wish we could help out more, but our spirits are calling," said Tucker. The ghosts faded away into the afterlife, where they were greeted by their spirits and their family members again.

"Tch, bitch ass ghosts," muttered Andre. "I guess I have to deal with you on my own."

"It would appear so, kid. So, ready to dance?" said the man.

Andre put his staff in front of him. The demonic man casually cracked his neck and said, "You wanna explain what you're doing in the Noctus Zone?"

"I should be asking the same question of you, demon," said Andre defensively.

"Name's Donovan. I suggest you start using it if you don't want to end up with another prosthetic arm," responded the man.

"You can't fool me, demon. I know what you're all about," said Andre as he pulled out his cross necklace.

Donovan sarcastically flinched and said, "Oh no. A little cross. I'm so terrified. I thought I couldn't fool you." Donovan took a few steps forward, unfazed by the cross. Usually holy symbols like the cross repel demons but it had no effect on this man!

Andre put his cross away and moved back as the man come closer to him. He yelled, "W-What are you?"

"Yeah, you might want to rethink your little theory about me being just a little jobber demon," said Donovan. He easily slashed though the Noctus Zone with his blade, causing it to dissipate; they were now on the roof of the complex.

"I get it now . . . you're a cambion, a half-demon," said Andre.

"Now you understand. None of that Cain-and-cross bullshit works on me. And judging by that thing on your arm, I get it now, too. You're one of those Scar-li-homun worshipers," said Donovan.

Andre replied, "What? I'm not one of those—" SHING!

With lighting fast speed, the demonic man rushed forward at Andre, barely giving the mage less than a second to block Donovan's sword with his staff. "Those are some quick reflexes, you got there. Not bad for a human," said Donovan. He swiped his sword down and Andre struggled to stay on the defensive. As Donovan continued to be on the offense, a tough battle ensued. Donovan continued to slash and dash at the young mage, who kept blocking the hits with his staff. Don headbutted Andre with such force that it stunned him. Had it not been for Andre's mask, his skull probably would have been cracked. While Andre was still stunned, Donovan's hand blazed with blackened hellfire. Donovan intended to hit him in the chest with it; however, Andre used the Yonica to grab his hand and emitted blue spirit fire, which canceled out the hellfire. Andre swept Don's leg and summoned an ice spear from his hands and attempted to stab Donovan in the face. Don rolled out of the way and swept Andre's leg back. Andre fell flat on his ass.

"Not bad," said Donovan as he got up. "Not many people can deflect my flames."

Andre pulled mana tethers out of the air using the Yonica. A solid wall of mana fell on Donovan and then dissipated. Andre willed lightning to his side and shocked Don while he was down, creating burns all over his body, but they swiftly healed. Andre panted and thought to himself, *I can't keep using all of this powerful magic and not experience feedback for it later.*

"This was my favorite coat! You'll pay for that with your life," said Donovan as he ripped off the tattered and charred sleeves of his coat. The demonic man picked up his sword and Andre thought to himself, *All right, so he's a sword user. If I find a way to get his sword away from him, then he'll be defenseless—*

BANG! Andre fell to the ground with a heavy thud. The barrel of the gun in Donovan's hand was still smoking. *When did he pull that out?* thought Andre. Andre had barely avoided a direct hit as he had hastily cast a shield up for his body; his mask alone wouldn't have been able to deflect the shot.

Donovan laughed and said, "Did you really think I would come into a fight without a strap?"

Andre shakily brought up his arms in an X shape and cast the spell "Aegis!" A pale purple shield surrounded him in a circle; he drew upon the Core of the Yonica to do this. *I have to call Ginny somehow*, thought Andre.

"Hahaha! Defensive magic now? Negro, please," said Donovan as he gripped his sword by the blade with two hands. With a mighty swing that would make any pro baseball player jealous, the pommel of the sword shattered the shield with no effort.

"H-How the hell?" said Andre, he attempted to cast the spell again, but Donovan grabbed the young mage by the throat.

"Dwarven metal, of course. If it's used right, it can rip right through defensive magic like tissue paper," said Donovan, who increased the pressure of his grip on Andre's throat. The young mage lifted the Yonica to blast Donovan in the face with all his might, but it was barely responsive to his commands. The demonic man yanked off the arm and chucked it to the side. "If Nightingale manages to get your ghost somehow, let him know this: I'm coming for him," said Donovan as the nails on his free hand began to grow to a sharpened point.

In a last-ditch effort, Andre opened his Space, the reservoir of a living being's soul to where a few small items could be stored. He pulled a gun out of thin air and unloaded into Donovan's face, causing the cambion to let go and reel back in pain. Andre growled, "You're not the only one who came to this fight strapped." Andre's mask fell off, but Donovan could not see the young mage. The hasty shots had partially blinded him—all was red and he was panting. Andre struggled to maintain his breath as well and willed the Yonica back to him; it used the hand to crawl back to him like a spider, and he reattached it. He pulled out another clip with a red mark on it. These were his silver bullets, supernatural killers. He reloaded the gun with the clip and shakily stood back on his feet, keeping the gun pointed at Donovan. Andre felt the influence of the Titan Lun course through his veins; he began to glow with a dark blue aura, his eyes blazed, and a crescent moon shone on his forehead.

Donovan looked up, his eyes healed enough to see, and said, "Thaddeus?"

Chapter 28

"Thaddeus? That was my dad's name! H-How did you know that name?" asked Andre.

Donovan shook his head and said, "No, no. Shit…fuck! Damn it! Israfil was right!"

"Cut the shit! How the hell do you know that name?" yelled Andre, keeping the gun locked dead on Donovan.

"You're not him . . . you look like him; you're . . . Andre, his son," said Donovan. He dispelled his sword, it disappeared in a haze of black flame.

Andre aimed at Donovan's heart, "How do you know my name? How do you know my dad's name? If this is your demonic bullshit, I'm going to fucking kill you—"

"He was the previous Moonchild in this area . . . your dad. He was my friend," said Donovan.

Andre laughed. "Bullshit. My dad would have never been friends with a demon."

"You don't know shit about your pops then. He was my friend. One of my best friends," said Donovan. He pulled out a picture and took off his mask.

It was a photograph of two men, one of them was Donovan and the other was Andre's father in his younger years. He had a Jheri curl, a turquoise and magenta jacket, eyes brimming with pride, and a cigarette in his mouth. Andre was shaken; he put down the gun and said, "H-How?"

Donovan coughed up some blood and said, "I know you probably have a lot of questions, kid. This is all a shock, believe me. I didn't think Thaddeus's family was still alive. After that car crash . . . I didn't know any of you survived. I looked. I swore to your father I would protect you guys after he passed. I thought I had failed."

"What the hell is going on up there? Andre, do you copy?" said Ginny over Andre's communicator. Andre looked at Donovan for a moment; he had recovered enough to move effectively.

"Look, kid. I'm sorry you got involved in all of this. I know you have a billion questions, but I can't be here right now," said Donovan.

Andre hesitated for a moment but finally said to Ginny, "The wraith is dead. Mission accomplished. Over." Andre placed the gun back in his Space. He had fallen to his knees. "Thank you, Andre . . . I really do mean that," said Donovan.

Andre was silent, still in shock. "Look, do me a favor; take this card" said Donovan. He put a black card in Andre's hand. It had a number on it. "Text me on that, it's a burner number. We'll meet up so I can explain all of this to you," said Donovan.

Andre put the card in his pocket and replied, "Donovan . . . I don't know you and I don't trust you."

"Heh, you really are your father's son. He said that to me, too, when we first met," said Donovan.

"Wait, before you go, look at me in the eyes," said Andre.

"Let me guess; you're going to sense my aura to see if I'm telling the truth," said Donovan.

Andre nodded. "Did you know my father?" asked Andre.

"Yes." A golden aura flushed around Donovan—he was being truthful.

"Did you kill him?" asked Andre.

"By The Existence, no! But the people that did . . . I killed them," said Donovan. A golden aura once again.

"Can I trust you?" asked Andre.

Don replied, "Can I trust you?" A grey aura flushed, which means that the question is inconclusive.

"All right, I'll let you go for now. If you're lying to me, I will kill you. Do you understand me?" said Andre.

"I do. I'd kill myself if I again broke the promise I made to your father," said Donovan. Donovan put his mask back on and jumped from the building.

Andre was still on his knees, in shock; he began to tear up. Ginny kicked through the rooftop door with assault rifle in hand, "Andre?! Andre?! There you are! Are you okay?"

Andre wiped away his tears and said, "Uh, yeah. That was just a rough spirit. Terrible time. I'm fine."

Ginny asked, "Are you sure? I can tell when you're lying to me, you know. I just wanted to make sure you're okay."

"I'm fine, Ginny. Let's just clean this crap up and get out of here," said Andre as he picked up his staff. He winced in pain; physically and mentally, he was distressed and so much was happening in his life at once. A link to his past . . . a link to his father . . . What would Andre do? There were so many questions in his mind.

Andre closed his car door and Nahid said, "Well, someone looks like a pile of dung."

"Fuck off. I'm not in the mood for your bullshit right now," said Andre as he buckled himself.

"What else has changed?" asked Nahid.

"Seriously, I am not in the mood. That mission was fucked," said Andre.

"Did a mortal die?" asked Nahid with a cynical tone.

"No, I-I got into a fight with one of my dad's friends. And he's apparently a fucking cambion. No one made mention of this to me. I don't know what to do with this information. And I just let him go . . . left him to his devices. He gave me a number to contact him by," responded Andre, his head hung low.

"I see . . . well, be careful then. Demons are a shifty sort. They have a way of manipulating things for their own benefit. It is in their nature," said Nahid.

"I know, I know. By The Existence; this is fucked . . . let's just go home already. I want to just forget that today even happened," said Andre.

Back home, Frederica said, "Oh, Master, you're back! How did the mission go?"

"It went well. But I'm in a lot of pain," said Andre.

"Oh no! Do you need me to tend to your wounds?"

"Sure, if you can heal emotional pain . . ." said Andre.

"Oh. Well, I think that talking works best for that," said Frederica as she beckoned him to the sofa. She gently placed her hands on Andre's body, applying magic to his wounds. "What's going on, Master? Why are you so upset?" asked Frederica as she moved her hands around the bruised part of Andre's lower back. The purple wound slowly faded back to a healthy shade of light brown.

Andre explained to her what happened with Donovan and the mission. Frederica gasped, "But he's a demon! How can you be so sure?"

"We did the test. He passed. If he was lying, it wouldn't have worked. Plus, he had this photo of him and my dad. I'm so confused," said Andre.

"I'm sorry Master . . . would you like me and Fred to attend your meeting with this Donovan character?" asked Frederica. She gently placed her hand on his neck and applied magic to where Donovan choked him.

"Yes, I would like that, but do it in a discreet way. No need to rouse suspicion to him," said Andre.

Frederica's ear twitched. "Yeah I know how to be discreet, Fred. Jeez. Also, Fred says he's sorry you're going through so much right now."

"Thank you both. I don't know what I'd do without you two," said Andre. Frederica nodded and smiled as she continued to heal Andre. After a thorough healing, Andre went to bed.

Chapter 29

Donovan slammed the door to his truck and yanked off his mask and sighed. "I told you that the son of Thaddeus and your paths would intertwine," said Israfil, now in the backseat.

"Yeah, yeah . . . I know. But why? Why did I not know this? How is little Leunis still alive?" said Donovan.

"Through means beyond your knowledge. The Lord has a plan for him as well as you. And for the time being . . . your paths must intertwine," replied the angel.

"I have so many questions: Is Natalie still alive? How about little Marsha?" asked Donovan.

"They are beyond this Earthly plane. That much I can tell you," said Israfil. Blood leaked from Donovan's forehead, his forearm's wound slowly pushed out bits of charred leather to repair burnt tissue. "Are you all right?" asked Israfil.

"Yeah, you know me. Most of this will heal by morning," replied Donovan. He pulled off the charred jacket and pulled out a shirt from the backseat and put it on quickly.

"What do you say we grab a burger?" asked Israfil.

"In all the centuries I've known you, you have NEVER said that once," said Donovan.

"I know, but it is on your mind," said Israfil.

"Stop reading my mind! You might go too far and see some stuff you don't want to see," said Donovan.

"I never dig that far, Aban," said Israfil.

Donovan asked, "Can you tell me this? Will this end in me breaking my promise to Thad again?"

"I only know what the Lord lets me know. I will say this—trust your instincts and exercise caution," said Israfil.

Donovan replied, "As vague and ominous as ever . . ." They got food from a nearby drive-thru.

At a nearby hill, Donovan and Israfil sat down on the open hatchback of his truck. Israfil had assumed a humanoid form consisting of a male of indeterminate racial background with brown hair and a five-o'clock shadow. On the tailgate, the duo ate the burgers. "So, what is your next plan from here?" asked Israfil as he folded the burger wrapper.

"Step one: I had a burger. Step two: I don't fucking know," said Donovan.

"I see . . . well, I am here if you need to talk," said Israfil as he put the folded wrapper back in the greasy bag.

"Talk about what? The fact that my dead best friend's son has been running around and I don't even know about it?" said Donovan.

"Indeed. I am can sense your confusion to this situation. But there is some good to come out of this. You know the truth now," said Israfil.

Donovan laughed and replied, "Sometimes I feel like all the truth does is get you hurt in the end. Where do I even begin to try and make this right? How do I get Leunis Jr. to trust me? I am a demon after all. You saw how he reacted." Donovan fashioned a ball of hellfire in his hand; it crackled.

Israfil placed his hand over the ball of hellfire and easily extinguished it. The angel replied, "Trust is something that is earned. Much like the growth of a tree, it takes time for it to be nourished and grow to a mighty oak."

Donovan rolled his eyes and replied, "Don't you start with that parable nonsense. I literally lived my initial years on this kind of stuff, listening to that junk on repeat."

Israfil let out a hearty laugh and replied, "I know. But it is in my nature. I've tried to do my best over the years to keep you safe. Regardless of your path in life. It is the promise I made to your mother long ago."

"I know. I still don't understand how my mother, a daughter of Eligos, was buddy-buddy with an angel. How did that even come about? Unless one of God's big birds isn't as holy as he says he is," said Donovan with a raised brow.

"Nonsense! It's a long story; one day when you are old enough, perhaps you will realize why that is," said Israfil as an owl began to hoot.

"But why? Demons and angels are supposed to be opposites—we're bad, you're good. That's the way it has always been," said Donovan.

Israfil placed a hand on Don's shoulder and said, "And as I keep telling you, half of your lineage is human as well. You don't have to live as a demon. I can see the good in you, despite your follies. You have lived your entire life swapping sides and I think there is a time when you realize that you must pick a side. And stay on it. I think this time with Andre Leunis will change you for the better. You will come to realize things that you never had thought of before. And as he influences you, you will change him as well. But keep in mind as you change him . . . will you be able to keep your promise to Thaddeus Leunis?"

Donovan let out a heavy sigh. "Great, now I feel like I have the weight of the world upon my shoulders," said Don.

"You will be fine. The Lord will never give you a load so great that you will not be able to bear it," said Israfil.

"There you go with that again . . . can we just leave religion out of our conversations? It's . . . too painful to think about the past," said Donovan.

"You may have given upon the Lord, but he has never given up on you, Aban," said Israfil.

"Heh, I try to stay out of the Big Man's way as much as possible," said Donovan.

"I must go. The Lord has tasked me with something else to do," said Israfil as he got up from the truck's tailgate.

"Where to?" asked Donovan.

"China," said Israfil.

"You must save thousands on travel with being one of The Existence's messengers," said Donovan.

Israfil laughed once again, a joyous smile upon his face. "Indeed. You will find the way, Aban. Just do not give up. And do not lose heart," said Israfil.

"You got it, Big Bird," said Donovan. The angel sprouted wings, which shimmered with a holy glare, and flew off into the sky, vanishing high above the clouds.

Donovan got a text from the employer of the job he took, "Any news on Nightingale's status?"

Donovan replied back, "The koi are circling." Which is code for "not yet dead but working on it."

The employer replied back, "Then perhaps you should be speedier about feeding them. Or else you may end up with some dead koi."

"Cute. I'll get the feeding done," replied Donovan. He made a call on his regular phone. "Hey Adrian, think you could do me a favor? I need a few nightmare demons. For what? Oh, I just need to invade someone's dreams," said Donovan.

Chapter 30

Andre was in the realm of dreams known as the Dreamscape. As a Moonchild, he could control his own dreams and reach out to individuals in their own dreams. In his dream, he sat down at a nice tree, taking in the scene of the sun setting. He had his arm back and wore a flannel shirt and jeans. He drank a lemonade as he sat next to his father Thaddeus, imagining what it would be like to talk to him again. Then suddenly, dark clouds expanded over the sunset, turning the sun blood red. The skies crackled with orange red thunder, a loud boom and gust of air washed over him. Out of the clouds, Donovan flew down in front of Andre using his wings. His wings were bat-like and greyish-brown in color. He retracted them back into his back, as if they were never there before.

Andre immediately grasped ahold of Donovan using the Earth around him. It held Donovan tight as if he were being held by two gigantic hands. Andre yelled, "What the fuck are you doing here?!"

Donovan spat out some dirt and said, "Relax, I'm not here to hurt you. I have an idea. Could you let me down?"

"I'll hear you out, but I'm watching you, dammit. What's your idea?" replied Andre.

"Dream invasion of the guy . . . Hunter Nightingale, Jr., the cult leader," said Donovan.

Andre asked, "You know the name of the cult leader? How?"

"If you let me down, I'll tell you what I know. Or you can just go back to chilling with that pale imitation of your father over there," said Donovan.

Andre thought for a moment and then finally replied, "Alright." He dropped Donovan and the dream's shape changed and the clouds were now a light blue. He summoned a table and two chairs. "Speak," said Andre.

"Are you familiar with dream raiding?" asked Donovan.

"Yeah, I've done it a few times before. But you need an item of said person to invade his—or her— dream," replied Andre.

"Wrong. There's more than one way to raid dreams" replied Donovan. Donovan pulled up a picture from his memory: a photo of teenager Hunter Nightingale and showed it to Andre.

"He looks kind of young to be a cult leader, doesn't he?" asked Andre.

"It's the last known picture of him. Nightingale prefers to stay in the shadows," replied Donovan.

Andre took the picture and with a simple will of magic, he and Don were lifted into a clear bubble amongst the

Dreamscape. There were several other bubbles in the hazy void of the realm. Each bubble represented a person's dreams and consciousness. Andre focused on the name "Hunter Nightingale" and three bubbles brimmed with a blue energy. "Well look at that, we got lucky. There's only three to search through. But how are we supposed to get in there?" asked Andre. He tried to go into the bubble, but he could not get in.

"And this is where nightmare demons come into play," said Donovan. He whistled and suddenly a swarm of nightmares came forward, their scrawny black fly-like bodies flying to Donovan.

Chapter 31

The nightmares proceeded to screech in a bat-like sort of howl and invaded the first Dreamscape bubble, spreading their negative energy into it. Donovan whistled again, causing them to only leave the way open for them.

"You're using demons to invade their dreams? Isn't this dangerous?" asked Andre with a raised brow.

"Relax, it's just a nightmare. If they freak out too much, they will just wake up. The worst that'll happen is that they'll think of how bad that dream was. But that also means our chance at finding clues will go poof, so we have to treat lightly," said Donovan.

"How often do you do this sort of thing?" asked Andre.

"Fairly often, depending on the circumstances. I've lived long enough to know that our inner self unveils some of the darkest secrets. Now come on, let's go," said Donovan as he jumped inside the bubble.

Andre changed his clothes into a simple armor and cloak and jumped inside the bubble as well. He lands face first into a soft and bouncy pink bush.

Donovan was already standing up and said, "Look at this cutesy shit." Andre got up and stood next to Donovan—looking at the wide expanse of pink, white, and other frilly objects. In the distance, a little blonde girl was in a princess outfit, having a tea party with an elephant that blew soap bubbles out of its trunk. "Approach carefully . . . follow my lead," said Donovan as he willed himself into a suit of pink and purple knight armor.

Andre did the same and asked, "So we're knights?"

"Yup, follow me." They walked down the hills and Donovan stood at attention in the presence of the little Queen. Andre emulated Donovan's posture. "Greetings, O Brave Knights," said Princess Hunter Nightingale.

"Greetings, your Excellency," said Donovan in an impeccable English accent, "We have slain the mighty Marsh-Mellow giants of the Honey Caves as you have ordered. Are the Queen and the King around?"

"Mommy and Daddy? I mean, King Thomas Nightingale and Queen Marianne Nightingale? They are not here. I shall report to them," said Princess Nightingale.

"Shit . . . I don't think this is our guy . . . our guy's a junior," whispered Donovan to Andre.

The princess gasped, "You said a swear word! That's not allowed! I forbid it!"

Suddenly, Donovan felt a bandage over his mouth, and gave a muffled sigh. The nightmares shook the bubble and the dream began to shake as well. "Hey! What are you guys doing?!" yelled Donovan to the demonic creatures. The nightmares pumped more negative energy into the bubble, causing the once-peaceful creatures in the dream to transform.

Ogres, orcs, and other boogeymen began to surround the three of them. Princess Nightingale screamed and said, "Please protect me, O Brave Knights. I'm scared!"

"It's okay, kid—I mean Princess. We won't let you get hurt, I promise," said Andre as he placed a protective ward around the frightened little girl.

Donovan willed into his hand his silver sword and easily struck down a shambling creature. *I need to bring these nightmares back under my control*, thought Donovan as he cast a barrage of hellfire fireballs at the monsters. He then slashed a fearsome beast, then another and another. Andre cast ice spikes to shoot up and impale several other beasts that approached. "There's so damn many!" said Andre.

"Swear!" said the Princess.

"This will keep up unless I get the nightmares back under my control! Keep that kid safe, I'll be back!" said Donovan as he ran out toward the edge of the bubble. He sprouted his wings and flew to the bottom of the bubble. He strapped his sword to his hip and stabbed his way under the bubble. The nightmares were being pulled into a vortex by a red tendril of some sort, being used against their will to induce a night terror. *What the hell is that?* thought Donovan. He set a dagger alight and chucked it right at the tendril. It let out a ghastly screech and it retracted into oblivion. The nightmares surrounded Donovan again and he commanded them to stop the night terror.

Donovan flew back into the bubble where Andre had shielded himself and Princess Nightingale. "You two okay?" asked Donovan as he retracted his wings and dispelled the armor.

Andre was already back in some regular clothes and Hunter said, "Thank you, Brave Knights! I don't know what I would have done without you both! That was so scary!"

"No problem, little lady. So . . . your parents' names are Thomas and Marianne?" asked Donovan.

"Yeah, I love them so much! Do you guys want to have a tea party with me?" asked Hunter.

"I'm going to have to take a rain check on that," said Donovan.

"Same here" said Andre.

"This is such a crazy dream; it's almost like a movie that Daddy and I watched together," said Hunter.

Andre whispered to Donovan, "So . . . any other bright ideas besides endangering children?"

"It wasn't that bad—she just would have woken up and maybe went crying to her parents. Relax, Little Leunis; I know what I'm doing," said Donovan. Andre and Donovan wave good-bye to Princess Hunter.

Hunter giggled and waved back at them, "Goodbye! Don't be strangers! You're always welcome back here."

As soon as Donovan and Andre left, Princess Hunter dropped the illusion and said, "Damn it! Lord Scar-li-homun, who are these interlopers who seek to interfere with our plans?"

The elephant replied, "A Moonchild and a Nephilim. But do not worry, my faithful servant; they shall not get far. Little do they know that I have manipulated the Dreamscape to ensure they cannot leave. I leave this duo to you to defeat. Do this in my name."

"It will be done, my Lord. They will not get far—my student shall obliterate them," said Hunter. "Are you prepared, Cindy?" asked Hunter to his faithful acolyte Cindy.

"I am, Master. I have prepared the trap for them in the second Bubble," she replied. Hunter and the young woman yelled out the words, "For the Fester of the World!"

Chapter 32

Donovan and Andre entered the second bubble where there was a young scrawny man. He wore glasses, had blonde hair, and was dressed in a hoodie and jeans. He was panting frantically and his eyes were wide open. "I don't think this is our guy," said Andre.

"Don't ever assume. Looks can be deceiving," said Donovan.

"I know, but still . . . he looks pretty jumpy and anxious. We should proceed with caution," replied Andre.

"HEY! Nightingale! We need to ask you a few questions!" yelled Donovan.

"Ah! I'll have the assignment by tomorrow, professor! I promise; just—just give me some time!" said the young man as he ran away from Donovan. The library's layout changed, and a wide bookshelf erected itself in front of the duo.

"Damn it, Donovan!" said Andre.

"Relax, it's his dream—he can't outrun his own dreams," said Donovan as he punched through the bookshelf. Andre and

Donovan jumped through the hole he made and chased after Nightingale. More bookshelves began to rise, and Donovan said, "This is getting us nowhere. We need to go up!" said Donovan.

Andre levitated up while Donovan flew up. The entire library was like a maze. The duo flew over to the bright lights of computers. There were a few other students—presumably Hunter's friends or just people from around his campus. They were like mindless zombies glued to the light of their monitors, endlessly clicking away at the keyboards. Hunter was at one of the computers, "Come on! Come on! You can do this . . . you're halfway done. You can't fail this class, you can't! Your family will hate you if you fuck up this opportunity for yourself!" he said to himself.

"Hunter Nightingale!" said Donovan with a bit of a snarl. He jumped out of his seat,

"Professor! I—" Donovan picked him up by the shirt. "I ain't a professor!"

Andre ran up to Donovan and said "Easy, you don't have to manhandle the poor guy." Donovan put him down and Hunter adjusted his glasses, "Sorry for running. Your friend here just bears a striking resemblance to Professor Smith. It really spooked me. He's infamous for being extremely merciless on assignments. I didn't mean to run—my anxiety just got the better of me. I haven't been doing so well in his class. If I don't pass his class . . . my parents will be so disappointed. I did very well in high school, but lately college has been hard. It's my first year and I just want them to be proud of me." said Hunter.

Andre says, "I'm sorry to hear that. I hope you do well in it. Honestly, we are here to investigate the Scar-li-homun murders—AH!" Andre got hit in the arm by a knife!

Donovan unsheathed his blade and a femininely-shaped, shadowy figure came from behind one of the bookcases. She kicked Nightingale out of the way and drew out dual daggers. She tried to kick Donovan but he grabbed her by the leg. He then threw her into one of the bookshelves. "Are you alright, Andre?!" said Donovan as he ran over to him.

Andre pulled the knife out of the prosthetic, "I'm fine. She only got the Yonica."

The shadow figure said, "Hmph, you guys are tougher than you look. But you will not stop Master Nightingale's plans!"

The mindless students began to twitch and contort before taking on much more monstrous shapes. Hunter began to hyperventilate again and Andre sighed, grabbed the young man by the arm, and they ran. Donovan pointed his sword at the woman, to which she replied to by laughing then she flashed a psychotic grin. The woman somersaulted into the air and chucked several daggers at Donovan. He simply swatted the daggers again with two powerful swings of his blade. When Cindy landed, she withdrew two more daggers and slashed at Donovan over and over like a maddened animal. Donovan deflected the attacks of the woman and managed to get in a good punch. The punch knocked off her hood, revealing her face. Cindy spat out some blood and used the power of Scar-li-homun, summoning tendrils into the dream.

After getting on top of one of the bookcases, Andre said to Nightingale, "This is your dream, man. You don't have to dance to the nightmare's tune! You have the power to stop this!"

Nightingale stammered, "B-But—"

"No buts! I'm going to put you into what is known as a lucid state, which should allow you to control the dream. Are you ready?" asked Andre as he willed a medallion into existence. He swung it back and forth and said, "Focus on the medallion . . . back and forth, back and forth." Nightingale became entranced by the medallion. "This is all a dream," said Andre. "You control it; it does not control you."

Nightingale felt himself grow drowsy until he fell unconscious for a moment. Then he woke up, much more confident than before. He took off his glasses and said, "You're right—let's kick some ass." His hands glowed with a mysterious energy and they both flew back to the battle. Donovan began to get overwhelmed by the monsters and Cindy. He fell to the ground and Cindy pointed Donovan's own sword at him.

Nightingale fired a blast of energy at her, which knocked her into a brick wall that he willed into existence. He zapped the tentacles in his dreams and turned the monsters into animals of various species. "Did I mention that I'm a biology major?" asked Nightingale as he turned the animals loose on Cindy.

She leaped up and slit a rhino's throat while bisecting a monkey in half with her daggers. Nightingale summoned a horde of crows and had them target Cindy. Despite her best effort to fend off all the crows, she was knocked to her feet.

She exclaimed, "Scar-li-homun! Grant me more of your power to crush these fools!" Her eyes glowed menacing red and she used tentacles to pull all three of them out of the Dreamscape bubble. Cindy tossed them all into the third Dream Bubble, and then she jumped into it as well.

Andre, Donovan, and young Nightingale dragged themselves to their feet and in front of them was a tall shadowy figure. "Ah, excellent work, my pupil. Right into the palms of our hands. Lord Scar-li-homun smiles upon on us this day," he said.

"Hunter Nightingale!" said Donovan.

"In the flesh!" said the true Hunter Nightingale, his adult face obscured by shadows.

"Uh . . . me?" asked the younger Nightingale.

"No, not you, the shadow dude!" said Andre as he summoned his staff and charged a ball of energy in his Yonica.

Donovan willed his sword back to him and pointed it at the true Nightingale. The true Nightingale laughed for a moment before he said, "This is all that stands against me and my Lord's vision? Adorable." One of his eyes glowed a crimson red and the interior of the Dream Bubble changed to that of a fleshy interior with a several flesh pods on the wall. In these pods, spirits were contained in them. They were being siphoned like batteries for power to Nightingale. Nightingale summoned Nightmares and revenants to his side; their numbers equated to a small army.

"Kill them quickly, my love; we have reservations for two tomorrow," said Cindy to the revenant Arnold. Arnold smiled and nodded with a grunt and charged the trio.

The young Nightingale summoned up a horde of ravens inside the Dream Bubble and the ravens provided ample covering for the trio to postulate. "Nice work, Hunter!" says Andre.

"I don't know how long I'll be able to hold them with this—my head hurts . . . a lot!" said Hunter.

"Take it easy; he may be trying to eject you out of the dream. Or worse," said Donovan as he ripped and tore through several distracted revenants.

The true Nightingale yawned and snatched one of the ravens out of the air with a tendril. The bird began to rapidly lose feathers and screeched in pain as it was transformed into an infectious bird. "Did you forget? This is my personal Dream Scape, I rule this domain. You all merely trespass in it," he said as he let go of the raven. The raven flew and it immediately infected the rest of the other horde. The infection did not take long to spread, and the true Nightingale commanded the subjugated ravens to attack the trio.

"Everyone, get close to me!" yelled Andre; he put his arms in a crossed manner like in his battle with Donovan. He willed a shield over them to deflect against the birds as they hacked stomach acid and other visceral bile.

"Disgusting . . . " said Donovan.

"I don't know how long I'll be able to hold this. If you have a plan, Don, I suggest you come up with it fast and do it now!" said Andre as he strained to keep up the shield.

"Only one. On my count, drop the shield" said Donovan as he clasped his hands and began to build up energy in the form of black hellfire. He closed his eyes for a moment and circled with his palms to build up more energy. After about a minute, Andre gritted his teeth as he continued to maintain the shield against the vomiting, emaciated birds. "Ready? On three! three . . . two . . . one . . . NOW!" Andre quickly dispelled the shield, which allowed the birds a way in. They shrieked as they dived down at the trio, their claws extended and ready to strike!

Donovan released the energy out of his hands, which exploded into a half-sphere shape of fire; it pushed away and incinerated the initial flock of ravens. Then it exploded once more into several shockwaves of hellfire that burned the rest of the approaching flock to a crispy end. The true Nightingale grumbled and commanded the revenants to attack with a wave of his staff. The revenants pulled out chunks of their flesh that became weapons of hardened muscle and bone. Arnold fashioned a sword out of the bone of his arm, pointed it at the trio, and growled toward his fellow revenants, which led them to charge. Donovan deftly swung his sword around in a flurry of slashes that easily took out four of the enemy's numbers. Andre extended the length of his staff and proceeded to whack and smack several approaching enemies. He swiftly and deftly blocked their crude weapon strikes with his staff. He finished off his attack by building up energy in his hand with the Yonica. He then punched this energy into Arnold, which caused the revenant to fly back so far that he fell out of the Dream Bubble.

"Arnold!" yelled Cindy with a despaired cry. She turned her attention to Andre.

"You'll pay for that, you crippled whelp!" yelled Cindy as she pulled out her dual daggers.

"Crippled? I'll cripple you, you fuckin' brat!" yelled Andre as flipped her the middle finger with the Yonica.

Cindy was ready to run forward, but the true Nightingale put his hand in front of her. "Now, now, my protégé. No need to be so quick to let your emotions drive you. Lord Scar-li-homun would be appalled at your brashness. Behold his power!" said Nightingale as he tapped into the power of the ghosts with a wave of his staff. The ghosts let out a blood-curdling scream as power drained out of them and the interior of the Dream Bubble began to change once more. The ground shook and twitched several times before spires of flesh rose up! The trio struggled to maintain their balance and suddenly found themselves wrapped up by tendrils of flesh. Andre struggled and shook, but the tendrils would not budge. The young Nightingale attempted to summon more ravens to him, but to no avail. Donovan sprouted claws and attempted to slash the fleshy tendrils. They were too thick, so he tried to bite them off with razor sharp teeth. None of them could break free, not even Donovan with his immense strength.

Hunter willed two seats in front of the captured and sat down as Cindy sat down in the other. "Do not think of it personally that I am killing you all. You see . . . it is simply a necessary evil. I think of myself as a soldier killing in defense of his President. I think you Americans can understand that analogy, right? Shoot first, ask questions later? Luckily for you, I am not without mercy. I shall give you an ultimatum: join me or die," said Nightingale.

"Got any other plans, dream invader?" whispered Andre to Don.

"Just one more gambit up our sleeves . . . pinch yourself awake," replied Don.

"Great plan, except we can't reach ourselves," whispered the younger Nightingale.

"We can't, but Andre can," said Don.

Andre thought for a moment, but then nodded when he understood. Donovan spat in the true Nightingale's face and he responded by grabbing Don by the throat. He wiped the spit off his face and said, "I guess you're choosing to die, demon." He manipulated the veins in Donovan's neck to twist and convulse and Don screamed in pain.

Andre detached the Yonica and cast ice into the true Nightingale's face. It stabbed right into his eyes and he screamed in pain.

Cindy yelled "Master!" and inspected his eyes.

Andre cast fire to one of Donovan's top bindings and Donovan willed his sword to him and freed himself. He then freed the younger Nightingale and Andre of their bindings. "Pinch yourselves! Hurry!" said Donovan. The true Nightingale pushed Cindy out of the way as he cast a blast of red energy. Donovan defended against this by casting Hellfire against the true Nightingale's blast.

The younger Nightingale pinched himself first and disappeared in the blink of an eye. Then Andre, then Donovan. The younger Nightingale woke up screaming so loudly that it woke up his roommate.

"Dude, what the fuck?" said his roommate.

"Oh, uh sorry. Bad dream," said the young Nightingale.

Chapter 33

The morning that Andre woke up, Frederica and Fred were over him. "Master, did you sleep okay?" said Frederica.

"I'm fine. I was able to get in a few decent hours . . . but staying on the offensive even when you're asleep takes it out of you," said Andre as he yawned. He attempted to reach out with his nub and then remembered he only had one arm. "Oh yeah," and grabbed his phone with his only arm. He checked the time. It was about six a.m. "How long did you guys watch over me?" asked Andre.

"Approximately five hours," said Fred.

"Looks like I'm going to have to reach out to Ginny . . . things got a lot more complicated," said Andre as he called her up.

Ginny picked up and said, "Hey, Andre. What's up? You okay?"

"I'm all right, but I have something to tell you and you're probably not going to like it." He told her about Donovan and the Dream Scape.

At Andre's apartment, Fred opened the door in response to some very hard knocks. "Hello Ginny," said Fred.

"Hey Fred, is Andre here? Because I'm about to send him into the next life," replied Ginny. Andre sat at the island of his table and drank some juice. Ginny had that look on her face: her face was pink as cotton candy, a scowl that indicated 'I will rip you two', and her mouth was in a thin line. "You lied to me," said Ginny.

"I know. I don't feel good about it. You're my friend and I hurt you. I'm sorry. I really am. But I need you," replied Andre.

"Yeah . . . now that things are too big, NOW you need my help. How can you even trust a demon's word? Have you lost your fucking mind?" argued Ginny.

"Probably, but he's pretty much the only link that I have about my father, plus hunting down Nightingale is in this guy's best interests too," said Andre.

"Probably not for the right reasons. And is that the name of our guy?" asked Ginny, her expression changed from "the look" to surprise.

"Yeah, Hunter Nightingale, Jr. He's the guy behind the cult," said Andre.

"And how can you trust his word?" asked Ginny with an arched brow.

"We went into the Dream Scape together. We saw what he could do . . . he's definitely our guy," said Andre.

"He was able to find out what we couldn't in the last three months? Who the hell is this guy?" asked Ginny.

"He says his name is Donovan. That's all he gave me. Yet somehow . . . he seems all right. He saved my ass last night," said Andre.

"Tch, yeah. Right after he kicked it," remarked Ginny, "Don't pretend I didn't see those marks on your neck."

Ginny sighed and placed her box of donuts and coffee pitcher on the island. "You caught me in the middle of breakfast."

"You deserve a much better partner," said Andre as he grabbed a donut.

"Yeah, yeah. Eat up and let's go meet this Donovan character," said Ginny as she grabbed a donut. "You two can help yourselves, you know," said Ginny to Fred and Frederica.

Frederica quickly took a donut and gave the tiny redhead a half hug, "It's always nice to see you, Ginny. Thank you." She smiled and walked back to her book.

Fred turned his back to the donuts and said, "I don't need to eat. Neither does she."

"But they taste so good, Brother!" replied Frederica, a few bites already taken out of her donut.

"They're bad for you," replied Fred.

She shoved a donut in his mouth and he sheepishly backed away into the next room." Frederica whispered to Andre and Ginny, "He's totally eating it right now." The three of them shared a laugh over it. After finishing off what they could, Ginny drove them to the park. She was dressed a bit more casually than she usually would be: a baseball cap and a hoodie. Andre had his Yonica equipped just in case things went south.

"You're late. And you brought someone I don't know. In a fuckup competition, you would take silver. I'm being generous, you'd probably take gold," said the voice of Donovan as he leaped from a tree.

"How long were you up there?" asked Andre.

"Don't try to change the subject, Leunis Jr.," said Don with a finger raised at him.

"I'm right here, you know. The truth is we don't know if we can trust you. You just pop up into your late best friend's son's life unannounced and now you're all buddy-buddy, trying to help? Seems pretty sketchy to me," said Ginny.

Donovan looked down at her and replied, "You've got some fire, little woman. I can see why you're dating her. Never would have pegged you for the redhead type though."

"W-We're are not dating! We're partners!" said Andre, his face now slightly red.

"Our relationship is totally professional," said Ginny.

"Yeah sure. And I'm the Marquess of Queensbury. Come on," motioned Donovan. He led them to a secluded part of the park with tons of trees. He blew into a wooden whistle; the piercing sound of the whistle unveiled a portal with sprites flying around it.

"What is that?" asked Ginny.

"A portal to the Realm of Faeries—well, a part of it anyway. It's better if we talk here just to cut off any tracking magic Nightingale might have on us," said Donovan. Donovan walked through first and Andre and Ginny followed suit. Beyond the portal was a long path through a bunch of trees. "Stick close to me and just follow the path. You don't want to get lost here, trust me," said Donovan. Andre was pestered by several little sprites; they were somewhat like flies but far more of a nuisance. Andre shooed them away and as they walked the path, Donovan stopped them with his arm and said, "Hold up." He approached the wooden gate of an armored fairy, much closer to Donovan's size than the other faeries.

"Halt! State your business," said the fairy solider. Donovan pulled out a necklace with a glowing purple crystal on it. He tossed it to the guard, who inserted it into a hexagonal hole on a wooden block of sorts and it pulsed green. The solider tossed it back and Donovan responded, "War plans. With those two."

"Understood; it has been a while since you have been here, Hell Moor. You and your companions are permitted to enter but be warned. Break any laws and you will be subjected to the high-est penalties of our land," replied the fairy guard. He opened the gate, and the wood magically shifted up as he raised a glowing hand.

"Noted. Come along, you two," said Donovan as they walked with him.

Chapter 34

Don, Andre, and Ginny walked into a large foyer with large stone walls a light green color, and the ceiling was adorned by a purple crystal chandelier. In the center of it all was a long red carpet that went all the way from the entrance of the room to the far end of it. In the middle was a table with a stand a gnarled tree rooted into the ground. The table was round, and the chairs were lined with a blue velvety color. There were four chairs in total, arranged around the table like the four main directions: north, south, east, and west.

A servant, a young fairy woman, walked through with a tray of tea and cookies. She smiled and when Donovan nodded, she flew out of there without a word. "I wasn't aware fairies could be so friendly," said Andre.

"They can be to people who don't live their lives trying to capture and segregate them. Or worse. Have a seat," replied Donovan as he sat down at the north table. Andre and Ginny seated themselves at the west and east chairs respectively. Donovan poured himself some tea and ate a cookie. He pulled something out of his coat, a plastic bag with a human ear in it. Ginny and Andre immediately flinched and exclaimed. "What are you two jumping for? You act like you haven't seen a dismembered ear before," said Donovan.

"Well, yeah, but we don't just carry around body parts like a damn trophy!" yelled Andre.

"Where the hell did you even get that?!" asked Ginny.

"Both of you relax. I'm 'borrowing' it from the police station. This ear is the key to getting our guy. Check this out," said Donovan as he pulled out a police report. He slid it toward them and Ginny and Andre picked up the report.

"How the hell did you get all of this?" asked Ginny.

"Don't worry about that. Focus on the case," said Andre. They read the report and it went as follows: An officer and his partner were hearing noise complaints from an abandoned building. They entered said building and found what appeared to be people—under some sort of trance. They were suspected to be drug addicts. When ordered to disperse, one of the "zombie-like" humans threw an ax at the duo. After narrowly dodging it, the officer and his partner shot at the humans, but they seemed to be unfazed by their bullet hole wounds. After an immense scuffle, only one officer's body turned up, the head mangled as shown by the pictures accompanying the description. The other officer was still missing . . . all that was left behind was an ear that was shot off one of the zombies.

Ginny and Andre closed the report and Donovan said, "And the puzzle pieces are fitting. I suspect these 'zombies' are the revenant assholes Andre and I fought last night. I figured this ear here would be useful to a Moonchild like Andre."

Andre picked up the bag and sensed some residual energy of the revenant: a rotting corpse smell. "Yeah this definitely helps; luckily, I brought along my ingredients for a tracking spell," replied Andre. He whipped out a small cloth bag and spilled the contents: a little doll, some gloves, a needle and thread, and a slip of paper with the symbol of Samedi on it.

"Ah, you follow the voodoo standards? That's interesting," said Donovan.

"Yeah, my teacher is all about the Voodoo and stuff," replied Andre.

"Who would that be?" asked Donovan.

"Her name's Afenti. But that's all you need to know," said Andre.

"Ah okay. Hmm . . . that name sounds awfully familiar for some reason," replied Donovan. Andre put on his gloves, placed the slip into a slit on the cloth doll's mouth, took the needle in his hand, and carefully pricked the ear with it. He wanted to make sure not to get his fingerprints on the ear. He carefully extracted a bit of blood and a tiny bit of flesh with the needle. He stuck it into the center of the symbol. He said in Xhosa, "I call to thee, Baron Samedi. I call thee, Lifeless Man. Let me borrow your eyes." The doll began to shake, and Andre quickly sewed up the mouth of the doll. Eyes began to appear on the doll and Andre commanded, "Put your hands on the doll." Don, and Ginny put their hands on the little doll and saw through the hazy, greenish vision of the revenant in present day.

The revenant was trudging along, his memories sealed away from him, and every faint attempt to remember was clouded by darkness; his body moved beyond his own command. There was a faint bloodstain on his shoulder from where blood dripped after he lost his ear. There was a long hallway, with several portraits and paintings adorning the walls. It appeared to be a mansion. The revenant, Arnold, led the pack of the revenants to the inner hall. It glowed with an orange energy, crackling with power. Nightingale, along with the Fester, and his cult were located in an indoors balcony. An unwilling woman was brought before him and he slit her throat, feeding her blood and soul to the portal. "My mansion shall serve as the catalyst for the Rise of Our Lord," said a man, who was bald and bearded.

"Yes, Lord Scar-li-homun shall reward you handsomely for letting us use your abode, Harold," replied Nightingale.

"Shit, I know who that is," said Ginny in a whisper.

"What was that?" said Nightingale.

"You!" yelled Harold to the revenant. Nightingale waved his staff and said "Step forward. We have been spotted. I thought this place was secured." He threw a fireball at the revenant and the link was shattered! The doll exploded into fluff!

"How many times do I have to say this, Ginny?" asked Andre.

"They can hear you. Even if you whisper," replied Ginny while sheepishly twiddling her thumbs.

"So, who is it, Ms. Know-It-All?" asked Donovan.

"That was Harold Rogers, eccentric millionaire. He has been on our radar for a while now, but we could never come up with anything conclusive. I guess we're killing two birds with one stone with this operation," said Ginny.

Donovan said, "I see, I guess me and Andre will—"

"Oh no. You two have done enough on your own, and almost got killed. I'm not letting you go in alone. I'm getting a drone and we are scoping this place out before we do anything. Donovan, respectfully, I'm going to have to ask you to stand aside and let Status Quo take over from here. I don't know much of your history with Andre or his dad but this is our fight. Not yours," said Ginny.

"Bullshit. I'm going after Nightingale. I'm doing this, with or without, y'all," replied Donovan.

"By order of the LAW, I demand that you back down," said Ginny.

"You really think laws will stop me? I will not sit down and be talked down to by some little redhead—"

"Whoa, watch your mouth. That's my partner. She has a point. I say that maybe having her do her thing is a good idea. But Ginny, don't push away the only link left I have to my family. Let him help," said Andre.

"Fine," said Ginny as she got up. They left the realm with missions underway.

Chapter 35

After they left the realm of the fairies, Donovan drove back to his apartment. He turned on the light and inside was Eligos, sitting at his table. "What are you doing here, Gramps?" asked Donovan.

"The better question is what the fuck are you doing, Aban?" responded Eligos as he smoked a cigar.

"I'm not sure what you mean," said Donovan.

Eligos got up from his seat; he was currently in a more humanoid form, but still well over seven feet tall. He puffed up the cigar smoke and said, "You know exactly what I'm referring to. You're meddling in the affairs of a Moonchild again."

"What of it, old man? And he's not just some Moonchild, he's the son of Thad," said Donovan as he swatted away the smoke.

Eligos sighed and shook his head, "You're a disgrace to your kind. You're just like your damned mother."

"Hey! Keep my mother out of this!" yelled Donovan, his eyes glowing an intense purple.

"No, let's face facts. If she never fraternized with humans, you'd never have existed. And perhaps she would have been around to this day. And try as I must . . . you still decide to go down the same road as her and will ultimately die like her as well!" yelled Eligos.

"Don't start to act like you ever gave a shit about me or my mother. You only view me as a weapon—a pawn to be used in your ultimate agenda. Well, hate to break it to you, but I do as I please. I refuse to be your lackey," replied Donovan, "So what if I'm helping Thad's kid? I made a promise . . . that I would watch that boy. And I initially thought I fucked up. Yet somehow . . . I'm getting a second chance to do that. And I'm not about to let my best friend down again," said Donovan as horns sprouted from his forehead.

Eligos grumbled and said, "It's merely The Existence trying to get into your head and corrupt you to his side. I refuse to let you be dragged to that side."

"I'M ON NO ONE'S SIDE!" yelled Donovan before he breathed fire onto the stone floor. He then yelled, "I'M ON THE SIDE OF ME, MYSELF, AND I."

"We both know that's not true, and soften your tone, boy. I could eviscerate you before you could even react. Over 700 years old, yet you know nothing. You are but a child," said Eligos as he kept smoking.

"Get out of my apartment. Now," replied Donovan.

"Not until you cease this matter of helping the Moonchild. I refuse to let you," said Eligos.

"Funny, I guess we're just going to have to fight," replied Donovan as his fingers elongate into claws. Eligos took on a much more monstrous form and he took a swipe at Donovan but he simply rolled out of the way. Donovan then took out his sword, sprouted wings, and charged at his grandfather. Eligos easily smacked him against a wall and he fell with a mighty thud.

Israfil flew in and emitted a mighty flash of light with his wings at Eligos, temporarily blinding him. In his hand, he carried a trumpet and blew from it. It emitted a loud note that pushed Eligos back, hurting his ears. He shrunk down to a more human-oid form and pulled out a dagger and prepared to fight Israfil, but Israfil easily lifted him up in the air and put pressure on Eligos's windpipe. Donovan shakily got up and Israfil said, "You two know that fighting like this on Earth is against the pact. This battle should be taken to Hell. Not in some apartment. Luckily for the two of you, I have taken away the sound surrounding the apartment. So we don't have to worry about the authorities being called here." He helped Donovan to his feet with one arm and then dropped Eligos, who got up on his own.

"Of course, it would be you that shows up to interfere," said Eligos.

"When demons insist to fight on grounds that are not allowed, then I must intervene," replied Israfil.

"Nonsense, you always spring to the boy's aid. You always have since he was an infant," responded Eligos.

"I am his godfather. It is only natural that I seek to protect him. Especially toward your advances. Now leave. Or be obliterated, Fallen One," said Israfil.

Eligos replied, "This discussion is not over, merely subverted for now, Boy. You should not always expect the angel to come save you. You are a demon, bound to Hell no matter what you do in this world. And acts of kindness showing your inferior human side will never change that."

"Leave, Eligos. I shall not repeat myself," said Israfil. Eligos disappeared in a puff of smoke.

Donovan said, "I could have handled this."

Israfil sarcastically replied, "Indeed. You clearly had this handled."

"Don't give me that. Why are you really here?" asked Donovan.

"Let us sit and talk," said Israfil.

"You expect me just to calm down after that fight and listen?" replied Donovan.

"I expect you to try, Aban," said Israfil.

Donovan frowned and ultimately the two of them sat down. Israfil said, "So you are working with him on this murder case . . . how do you feel?"

"I feel a lot of emotions. But I'm setting them aside for now, at least until this Nightingale situation is over. When it's all said and done . . . I will talk to him. About everything. The kid deserves that," said Donovan.

"An honorable thing to do. My reason for being here was merely to tell you that the path you have chosen is not yet done. Much will happen. You run the risk of becoming truly fallen as you were in the past. Your time as James Helmore . . . was the closest I had ever seen you to this state. Take heed . . . do not lose yourself. Continue to rage against your demonic nature; fight it with all you can. I implore you. Please," spoke Israfil.

Donovan sighed and responded, "You will never let me live that down. I'll do what I can. But what I know for now is that Thad's son deserves better than he got. And I will watch over him with my dying breath."

Israfil laughed and said, "I shall hold you to that, Aban. I will be keeping my eye on you. Not merely out of necessity of my profession, but as your godfather. Your eyes . . . they're just like your mother's. I trust you to do the right thing."

Israfil flew through the roof with a smile and Donovan simply sighed and said, "What a mess . . . "

Chapter 36

"Oh, hi Master! How did your meeting go? I was just in one myself!" said Frederica, as cheerful as ever. She was holding a laptop, finishing a video call with her editor concerning her drafts.

"That's good, dear. It went well. Is Fred in the Garden?" asked Andre.

"Yes, he is!" said Frederica as her ear twitched, "Oh knock it off! My editors love it! I don't care if you think it's trite!"

Andre shook his head and walked past her. He walked up to the washroom door at the apartment, closed his eyes, and placed his hand on it. It glowed with blue energy and he opened it, revealing the Garden. The Garden was a realm in the Mana Stream, an interstice where sources of mana in the world existed. Each Moonchild had their own iteration of the Garden and it served as a foundation from which they could draw mana from as well as store things. Andre's version of the Garden just so happened to have various plants of magical origin that liked to grow there. He and Fred had collected several others over the years. He also housed an entire library of books about magical subjects as well as several reagents for making magical items. Fred was often in here, tending to the plants and keeping things organized. He was very efficient at it and in tandem with his eidetic memory, it made him one fearsome librarian. Fred was currently clipping and watering an Aesir sapling. He put down the can and said, "Ah, Master. You have returned. I'm glad to know that the meeting was a success."

"Thank you, Fred. So . . . have you looked at effective methods that would be useful in defeating Scar-li-homun? And revenants?" asked Andre.

"I have. I reviewed the *Invertum Respirum,* Vol. XIII you provided me with and have concluded that fire seems to be the more optimal method of dealing with both, as well as exorcism and containment," said Fred.

"I see; why don't we build a fire matrix for the Yonica as well as a bunch of those clay incantation circles containment?" said Andre. Fred nodded and quickly made his way to the bookshelf and grabbed two books. He quickly turned to the pages where the relevant information for these items were. He then came back with the ingredients as well as a cauldron and stirring rod. Andre replied, "Excellent work. Let's get started on those clay matrixes first."

The ingredients were all in mason jars, with quick little labels made with tape and a marker. The first was a jar of clay; clay was a versatile ingredient used in many matrix recipes. The next was a jar of soot. Due to its composition, it had to be handled with care; otherwise, it could cause respiratory issues. The last jar needed for this recipe was rosemary, a simple yet effective herb that wards away demons and spirits of all matter. Andre filled up the cauldron with water from a nearby hose in the Garden. He then focused and willed a small wisp of mana into his hand from the Stream and threw it into the water. This caused the water to purify and become a light blue. Andre then took a rolling pin to the clay, flattening it into a sheet for maximum surface area. He took a cup and cut about twelve circles from the sheet using it. Then he rolled it again and made as many circles as he could, resulting in about fifteen circles. He put the remaining clay back in the jar, which was about half empty now. Andre carefully sprinkled a pinch of soot into the mana-infused water, turning it into a shimmering black. He snapped off a small, stiff reed from the nearby small lake and whittled it with a pocket knife, bringing it to a sharp point. He then passed it to Fred and he perfectly memorized the symbol of warding from the book. Fred made an indent of each of the circles with the symbol of warding as Andre took a dropper and filled it up from the cauldron. He then dripped the ink substance into the indents, filling them up. Andre chanted a spell by saying in Latin, "Spirit begone," and the clay circles slightly glowed with energy. Fred put them into the oven to bake. Andre willed the remaining soot water to separate back into soot and placed it back into the vial. The remaining blue water was still ready for the next matrix. "Now let's get to work on that fire gem," said Andre.

Andre wheeled the cauldron over a campfire of sorts and stoked the flame. The mana water reached a boiling point and he stirred it. He then lighted a rose on fire, letting it burn to ashes to put into the cauldron. He took a small red salamander off a nearby tree and handled it a bit roughly to make it feel threatened. He held its little head and it spat out a little flame that he pointed towards the cauldron. The embers of salamander's flame were absorbed into the cauldron. The salamander hissed at Andre before calming down after he gently patted its head. Andre said, "Yeah, yeah, I know. I don't like it any more than you do." Andre fed the small salamander a bug and let it crawl back onto a tree. He consulted the book again and dropped in a small bit of charcoal. He then took some tweezers and pulled out a small fire ant from an ant colony. He dropped it into the cauldron and said, "Sorry little guy." Fred then handed Andre a clear oval-shaped crystal. He dropped it into the cauldron and sat down in a meditative pose. "I call upon Fyreon, Primordial Titan of Fire, Sister of Lun, to bless this matrix and grant me power over fire," said Andre. A small wisp invoked the fire and the cauldron's mixture turned into the color volcanic red. Andre stirred it again and the water quickly evaporated, burning the tip of the rod. After letting the water turn to vapor, a shimmering red fire gem was all that was left. Andre picked it up using his prosthetic and placed it on the table.

The egg timer dinged and Fred pulled out the clay symbols. The clays were now cooked red orange and the symbols had been burned into them. They were flat yet resilient. Harder than a brick. Andre put on the Yonica and pulled the blue gem out of the palm of it, which caused the whole arm to go inert. He placed the fire gem into the slot and the arm twitched to life once more, the theme no longer white and blue, but white and red. He tried it on. A stone floated in the Mana Stream. He summoned a spear of flame and chucked it at the rock; it exploded into more flame upon contact. Andre crumbled a blank piece of paper into ash, his fingertips glowing red. "Excellent work, Fred. Do you mind cleaning up for me? I think I'm going to make a call to Ginny and Donovan and tell them I'm ready," said Andre as took up the clay matrixes and put them into a cloth bag.

Chapter 37

Ginny walked through the halls of the Status Quo building and she heard a voice. "How's it going, Kravitz?" asked a gruff man.

"It's going all right, I guess. How about you, Schneider?" asked Ginny.

"It's been a long day, hunting down rogue snats" (short term for "supernaturals"). "Damn kelpies and the like, they strayed off their normal path and have been giving boat-goers some hell," said Schneider.

"Ah. I have a murder case to solve. Andre found an unlikely lead and we intend to pursue it," said Ginny.

"I see. Well, best of luck with that. And say hi to the family for me. What are they up to anyway?" asked Schneider.

"You know, the usual. Hunting down snats wherever. My mom and dad are in France; my brothers are in the Midwest," replied Ginny.

"I hope those knucklehead brothers of yours are staying out of trouble. I don't worry about your parents—they're too good at what they do. How's Leunis?" asked Schneider.

"Going through a lot honestly. But he'll get through it. He's strong," said Ginny.

"Yeah, that's a tough young man. Anyways, here is my stop. I'll see you around," said Schneider as he went into a nearby door.

"You take care, Schneider," said Ginny as she kept moving forward.

She approached the manager of supplies and he put down his newspaper; he was behind reinforced glass and ten-inch steel doors. "Ah, Kravitz. You're finally here. I have an XSIS-1040 charged up and ready to go for ya. Just need ya to sign for it," he said.

"No problem, Mike," said Ginny as she took the clipboard and signed her name: Harriet G. Kravitz. She passed it back to him and he slid open his hatch and put the drone case through one of the slots. "The container also functions as a power bank in case ya need extra juice. Good luck on the investigation," said Mike.

"Thanks . . . me and Andre are going to need to it," said Ginny as she walked out of there with the case in hand. She went to the rooftop of a building close to the mansion. She opened the case; inside was a black plastic and steel drone, its mini propellers durable yet light enough to fly. She took the cover off the little camera on its undercarriage and then turned on the controller; a screen connected to the drone's camera was in the middle. She turned on the drone with the press of a button; a little green light came on it. She allowed it to lift off. Propelling above her head, she slightly adjusted the camera. She turned on the cloaking tech, which the drone did by using specially made panels to refract surrounding light.

Ginny's drone could see traffic as well as any oncoming obstacles. The drone had a small gun on it, in case of danger. *Let's see what I can find out,* thought Ginny. She drove the drone into the yard of the mansion; the grass was lush and very well-kept, and it could fool anyone into thinking it was a good place. "What the hell have you gotten yourself into, Rogers?" muttered Ginny to herself. Harold Rogers was a tech mogul, who decided to sell off his company and live a lavish life, but when his wife died due to end-stage cancer, he began to isolate himself from others. There were rumors that he was involved in shady dealings, but soon those whispers stopped being passed around, allegedly due to him greasing the palms of the media and a few politicians at the White House. It wasn't much of a surprise that he was involved in the dealings of magical beings and snats.

The drone's camera adjusted on the wind to the window. She watched a revenant, a young brown-haired woman, through the window. "Come on!" yelled a revenant, a man barely out of his twenties, who dragged her away from the window by the arm. A few other shambling figures passed by.

"These things give me the creeps. All these dead people walking. It's not right," thought Ginny to herself, "Time to see if I can find a way in." The mansion was guarded by a lone revenant at the front, no weapon in hand—probably to not rouse public attention. He stood there, as stiff as a statue, unmoving, a vacant look on his face. Unlike the pale blue of the other walking corpses, his eyes were bland brown. Ginny moved the drone to the chimney; no smoke seemed to be going through it, so she maneuvered the drone to propel down it. The drone descended and then quickly rose up close to the ceiling. The living room was teeming with revenants, aimlessly roaming around without any purpose. Like wandering souls. A truly creepy sight. The room was dark, but a revenant called to them and gestured for them to come.

The drone followed the crowd of revenants, seemingly unaware of its presence to begin with. The revenants were led into an inner foyer, moving with the speed of cattle. Several black-robe-wearing figures, chanted to their Lord Scarli-homun. Nightingale was there. He was a pale, lanky man with dusky, brown hair tied into a ponytail at the top, the rest hanging down to his shoulders. He had one brown eye, one glowing red, a stubble beard, and he wore a cloak in addition to his grey V-neck shirt; he wore a necklace with two wedding bands. "Bring the sacrifice forward," he said in his British accent. A young woman had her wrists bound and she was struggling against her captors. As she resisted for a bit, Nightingale said, "Do not fear; rejoice. Your blood shall be spilled for one of the Great Ones that came before us. He and His Siblings shall bring in the new age. Have you made your peace with the False God?" He took off her gag and she cried for help, but it was too late. Nightingale slit her throat, and her blood dripped down the bannister and into the summoning circle on the ground.

Nightingale's red eye glowed and he turned to the drone. He felt Ginny's presence though the drone and laughed. He then said, "Ah, so you're one of the ones who were peering at the Beginning of the Greatness To Come. I don't blame you. It's a magnificent sight, isn't it?" Ginny stayed silent as she watched Nightingale walk down the steps. He was tossed his gnarled tree branch staff by Cindy, who was next to him the entire time. "Where are the other two?" asked Nightingale, "The cambion and the Moonchild?"

Ginny pressed a button to shoot at Nightingale, but a revenant ran in the way and shielded him from the shots. "You have spirit. Lord Scar-li-homun likes that. Oh," he sniffed, "The Blood of a Kravitz, even better." He cast a zoom spell that allowed him to bring Ginny to him. Ginny was disoriented by the sudden shift of her being but was swift enough to pull out her gun. A rat bit her hand and she was forced to let go of the gun. The revenant Arnold grabbed her by the throat and pinned her to the wall. He took her phone and gave it to Nightingale. He tapped on the phone and said, "Blasted passcode, what is it?"

"Up yours, you repugnant human being!" said Ginny. Arnold slammed her against the wall hard, knocking the air out of her lungs.

"Very well then, I'll do this the old-fashioned way. People don't ever realize how much hair from others gets onto them," said Nightingale. He precisely snagged a couple of hairs off her, brown in color.

Chapter 38

Andre met with Donovan at Ginny's office door; he opened it with his key but there was no one inside. "What the hell? Where is she?" said Andre.

"That's not a good sign, kid," said Donovan.

Andre tried calling her, but it kept going to voicemail. "Shit, she must have gotten captured," said Andre.

"I kinda figured that would happen. It was a dumb idea to send a drone in there in the first place. She's probably dead," said Donovan.

Andre grabbed him by the shirt and said, "Shut the fuck up. I know Ginny, she's not dead. They're not taking her without a fight."

Donovan slapped his hand away and replied, "She's a human ... going up against a bunch of revenants. She may be a Kravitz, but there's only so much those bastards can take."

Andre said, "Whatever. We need to raid that place, now. I'm going to call for backup. I'm going to make a tracking spell using a lock of her hair she gave me for emergencies, and—"

Andre felt a force on the back of his neck, the apparition of Nightingale appeared before him, with Ginny in hand. "Hello, the Moonchild, I presume?" said Nightingale, still in his shady form. Andre gasped, "Ginny!"

Donovan leaped up to his feet, "What the hell is happening?" Andre gripped his shoulder, allowing Donovan to see what Andre saw.

"Unfortunately, I could not simply call you on her phone due to your friend—Ginny, was it? —being disagreeable. Luckily, I found a few of your hairs stuck to her and cast a linking spell," said Nightingale.

"You son of a bitch," swore Andre.

"How rude—my mother was a saint. She did what she could for me. Until my father saw it right to command rats to eat her for wanting me to take him away from his abuses. Then I was left alone. Left to darkness. Until Lord Scar-li-homun showed me the way. But I digress. I have come to compromise. Join me and I may spare the woman. If not, I shall sacrifice her. Her blood would greatly please my Lord. Kravitz souls tend to be very . . . robust. She may even prove to be a worthy vessel. Take heed to my words, young man. You have twenty-four hours to make your choice. Ta-ta!" said Nightingale as he ended the link.

Andre was fuming; his eyes glowed blue for a moment and he was ready to storm out of there until Donovan grabbed him by the arm. "Hold up, kid. You can't just go in there guns blazing and expect to win," said Don.

"What do you care? You suddenly show up in my life and suddenly you think you're my friend? You assumed she was dead up to this point, so why should I listen to you?" replied Andre with hate in his eyes.

"Andre, hear me out," replied Donovan as he dragged Andre back into the office. He closed the door and sighed. "There is a lot of shit you don't know. And it's complicated. I'm sorry for what I said about your partner, friend, girlfriend, or whatever y'all got going on." Andre folded his arms; his eyes glowed blue once more. Donovan continued, "I promise to explain your father's past and whatever else you want soon. Very soon. From the past few days that I have known you . . . I know that you are a good person. You are nothing like me. I get that." Donovan closed his eyes for a moment and gave a gentle chuckle. "You're more like your father than you realize. Let's come up with a plan rather than ad-libbing something that could get us killed," said Donovan.

Andre's eyes went back to normal and he said with a heavy sigh, "Okay."

Donovan pulled out a map and said, "Okay I was able to get a map of the mansion. There are three levels to it. And two foyers: one on the outside and the inner one on the second floor. Third floor is made up mostly of bedrooms and a main office," said Donovan.

Andre pulled out his bag and shows him the matrixes. "These matrixes are used to ward off spirits and outright expel them. And I've also upgraded my Yonica with a fire gem. Scar-li-homun and revenants have a huge aversion to fire. I suggest you use that, too," said Andre as he passed a matrix to him.

"Why so little? We'll probably need more than this," replied Donovan.

"They're re-useable. Why lug around a bunch of them? That'll just weigh us down," said Andre.

"Really? I had no idea you could use them like that. I remember your dad lugging them around in a sports bag. Smart move," said Donovan with a smile.

After formulating a plan together, Donovan drank more of his soda and stood up, putting his hand on Andre's shoulder. "Kid, I'm sorry for not being there for you like I should have. I should have looked harder after that accident, if I had—" Andre said,

"You didn't know. It's all right, Donovan. Honestly, I don't know what is going to happen after we save Ginny, which we will, but whatever happens, I want to know the truth about my dad."

"Of course. But let's focus on saving Ginny for now," said Donovan.

Andre nodded and replied, "You're right.

Donovan said, "I have my blades; you have your magic stuff, and most of all, we've got a badass car."

"Damn right, Nahid! Get ready!" yelled Andre out of a window.

"Hey, asshole! Shut the fuck up!" yelled some random bystander.

"Hey! Fuck you!" yelled Andre back to the fellow as they flipped each other off. Donovan joined in on the flipping off the bystander until he turned the corner.

Nahid sighed and then said, "How did I end up in this mess?"

Chapter 39

A man of Jamaican descent wearing a black hat, rode in a cab. His head lowered as the cab drove to their destination. "So, I take it you're from the Carribean?" asked the cab driver. "I assume because of the accent." The man said nothing in response. The cab driver said to himself, " . . . okay then." He stopped in the park. The man paid the fare and walked on his merry way.

The year was 1989 during the springtime; there were bikers, runners, and families all about. The man walked through the park and took in the scenery. He became distracted and accidentally bumped into a man with a briefcase. "Watch where you're going!" yelled the British man, his brown eyes and furrowed brows detailing his annoyance.

"My apologies. This Palm will be more careful next time," said the man as he walked past him.

"Tch, fucking better . . . damn foreigners," said the British man as he quickly closed a clasp on his briefcase, which was slightly opened to reveal guns. What could this man be up to?

He took a seat at a bench with a brown bag on it: the sign that this was the meeting place. Another man, wearing sunglasses and a suit, approached. "You have what I requested, Nightingale?" asked the man.

"Depends—do you have my fee?" replied Nightingale vaguely. The man opened his briefcase a bit to reveal the money within it.

"Then the answer to your question is yes," replied Nightingale with a smile. He and the man swapped briefcases and lightly nodded to each other. They headed their separate ways. *Too easy, now to report back to the Boss; maybe this will be my chance to move up in the racket,* thought Nightingale.

Back at the hideout, The Boss talked to an associate concerning a package of sorts and Nightingale came in with a big smile on his face. "Ah, Nightingale, you're back. Has my merchandise been sold?" asked the Boss.

"Indeed it has, Boss!" replied Nightingale.

"Excellent! Boris, will you take that briefcase from him, please?" asked the Boss. Boris took the briefcase and went to the back to count it. The Boss asked, "Fancy a glass?"

"Sure," said Nightingale. He poured them both a glass of whiskey and gave one to him before they both sat down. "I understand that you have been looking to move up from a runner to a launderer? Is that right?" asked Boss.

"Y-Yes, if you'd give me the opportunity, then I would not let you down! I'm capable, I can count, I can move units as well as you need me to," said Nightingale with a shaky confidence in his voice.

"Well, I'll see what I can do to make that happen for you," said the Boss. He drank.

Boris whispered something into his ear. The Boss frowned. "This bastard tried one of the oldest tricks in the book!" said Boris in his baritone, Cockney accent. He tossed the briefcase in question onto the Boss's desk, revealing that only the top layer of it was money—the rest was simply two books: one *Grey's Anatomy* and the other was without a title, old and bound in leather of mysterious origin.

"The fuck is all this, then? You little fuckin' worm," said the Boss in an almost disgusted tone. Boris grabbed Nightingale by the shirt and he said, "I-It wasn't me! I swear! It must have been the guy who bought the merchandise—"

"No excuses! You should have checked it before you dragged your sorry arse back here!" yelled the Boss, "Deal with him. Let this be a lesson to you. I will not stand for failure." Boris and another muscular man named Armando came in and beat the daylights out of Nightingale.

It was now night; Nightingale parked his car and trudged into his home. He turned on the lights. His wife Rebecca was seated in a chair, reading. She closed the book and said, "You're late."

"Sorry, my job kept me busy," said Nightingale.

She sighed and then rolled her eyes at him. "You mean your occupation where the employeers can beat you to a pulp when they like? I couldn't bare it if Hunter Jr. saw his father in such a sad, pathetic sake. You should be thankful he's almost asleep." She set down the book and said, "Well? Come on then—can't have you wishing him good night looking like you were dragged along the road." She carefully disinfected and bandaged his wounds. After she was done, she said, "Why can't you just leave this life? Why not make an honest living? My father owns a company—"

"Your father this, your father that. Fuck that lout. I aim to make my own way in the world. I refuse that bastard's handout," said Hunter Sr.

Rebecca replied, "Language! He can hear you, you know. These walls are thin. Think of our son; your actions not only affect you but us as well. You should do well to remember that."

"Right . . . " said Hunter in a solemn tone.

Hunter Sr. walked in and there was his little boy, Hunter Jr., sitting with a smile on his face. He was about four years old, auburn hair like his mother, brown eyes like his father, dressed in his pajamas. "Father, you're back from delivering packages?" asked the little boy.

"Indeed I am, Son. How was your day?" asked Hunter Sr.

"It was great! Me and Mummy watched cartoons and got to go the library today! See? It's a book about a doctor trying to cure an unknown sickness! Will you please read it to me?" asked Hunter Jr.

"Of course, but only if you promise to go to bed afterwards. A growing boy needs his rest," said Nightingale. He then play-fully ruffled his son's hair. He grabbed the book and read to his son about Dr. Stampolos as he struggled to try and find a cure for this silly disease that caused polka dots to appear on the patient. He tried balloon animals, seltzer water, and even a horror movie to try and scare the spots off. By the time Nightingale was finished reading, Hunter Jr. had fallen asleep. He kissed his son's forehead and turned out the lights. He gently closed the room door.

Hunter Sr. got into bed with his wife Rebecca. She was still reading her book from a series of novels based on a private investigator in the mid-1920s to late 1940s. "Is he sound asleep yet?" she asked, still reading the book.

"Yeah," said Hunter as he lay in bed.

She put the book down and said, "I worry about this family a lot."

"Me too," replied Hunter, "I love you both with all my heart."

"Then why do this to us?" asked Rebecca.

"I have no choice. I can't just up and leave this life like I want to. I know too much," said Nightingale.

"Then why not report it to the authorities?" said Rebecca.

"Then you two would be in great danger. I'll find a way out of this. Somehow. I love you. Very much."

Rebecca replied, "I know, love. I love you too." They kissed each other and turned out the lights before going to sleep.

Chapter 40

Donovan and Andre parked in a nearby building and got out. They were approached by a couple of people in the building. They wore casual clothing, but their eyes gave them away. "Fuck, they've been tracking us. Get ready for a fight," said Andre as he narrowly dodged some gunfire.

Donovan summoned his sword and swiftly dodged one of the revenant's gunfire. The male revenant reloaded the gun but Donovan easily sliced his head off before he could fire another round. But that did not stop him. The headless body of the revenant punched Donovan with great strength, knocking him to the ground.

Andre summoned his staff and twirled it around to summon a shield to deflect more gunfire. He used the Yonica to blast a javelin of fire at the other revenant. It pierced her easily and she exploded in a flurry of fire; her flesh was burning but she attempted to charge Andre. Andre chucked one of the matrixes at her and she fell to ashen dust. Her ghost was free and was about to pass on. But at the last second, Andre was able to grasp the spirit and he yelled to Donovan, "Donovan! Use this!" Andre tossed him one of the matrixes and Donovan bashed the headless revenant to dust using it. Andre grasped the other ghost and they were both clearly in distress when they realized what was going on. "Sorry to do this to you two, but we need another look at where other revenants will pop up," said Andre as he tapped into their memories.

He fast forwarded past their personal lives and delved into the point that they were murdered and the time they spent over the last couple of weeks as revenants. He pinpointed the "corpus rex" a young fellow by the name of Arnold. He looked to be about seventeen or eighteen; as corpus rex, he was the head revenant with a bit more power and influence than the average revenant. He seemed very involved with Cindi, that psycho from the Dream Scape. He had commanded a bunch of revenants at different outskirts of various buildings to attack Andre and Donovan and halt their advances toward the mansion. Andre briefly got a glimpse of Ginny being tied up and hanging above the summoning circle. "Thank you both," said Andre as he let the ghosts go.

"No thank you. Save the others. Please," they replied as they passed on to the afterlife. Andre felt them reunite with their spirits in the Afterlife.

Andre passed on the information to Donovan. He replied, "Well that's inconvenient. Any way to sever the link to Nightingale?"

"Nope. Not unless I could tune into the method being used to control them. It's probably Forbidden One magic if I were to guess. I could go insane if I even attempted to tap into that magic, or worse," said Andre as he felt a chill up his spine. He went on to say, "I'd end up like a puppet like Nightingale; these arrogant mages think they're hotshots for allowing some eldritch force to allow them their power. That power always comes at a cost." Andre shook his head and said, "Anyways, enough with the lecture. We are going have to hoof it the rest of the way on foot. Nahid, stay here, but attack and escape if you have to," commanded Andre.

"I'll take much fulfillment in running over any pathetic humans that would dare attempt such a thing," said Nahid while revving the engine. Andre attached two clay matrixes on the hood of the car and replied, "Good luck, buddy."

Donovan and Andre walked into the crowd before the cops came to investigate the gunshots; the last thing they needed was to take up precious time to explain to the cops about this investigation. The normal cops never would understand the inner machinations of the supernatural world and what happened in it. They always wanted logic and answers for every little thing that happened. They successfully blended into the crowd and speedily walked close. They were very close to the mansion; however, a revenant subtly pulled out a knife to stab them. Andre swiftly walked up to him and hit the revenant in the gut with the matrix, causing him to fall into an alleyway before evaporating into dust without arousing suspicion. "Nice move, Little Leunis," said Donovan.

They were almost to the mansion. A revenant in a hoodie looked to a colleague of his and gestured for him to follow the duo. "How are they keeping tabs on us so well?" asked Donovan.

"Nightingale's got my hair; he's definitely tracking me. If only I had a way to break the link, this would be so much easier than playing this cat and mouse bullshit. They won't try anything too big out in the open like this. It'd be a bad play on their part," replied Andre. A revenant approached from the rooftops, sniper rifle in hand and was dead on their trail. The light reflected off his scope. Andre and Donovan took a sharp turn away from the building to avoid getting shot. After several twists and turns, they finally made it to the mansion. Several revenants moved amongst the crowd to try and find them.

They approached the mansion by going through the side. Donovan lifted Andre up over the gate, narrowly avoided getting stabbed by the pointed tops of the gate. He ungracefully fell flat on his face and spat up dirt. Donovan backflipped, using his wings to further boost himself into the air and then lands down on the ground on both feet. "Showoff," said Andre as he brushed himself off.

Donovan said, "Your father used to say the same thing. Now let's go save your friend."

Andre lifted the Yonica to his eye and formed an "O" with his thumb and index finger to view a farther distance away than he normally could. "I only see one revenant by the main entrance.

Wait, more are coming out and they're armed with guns. Fuck, we better be careful," said Andre.

"More like you be careful. I'm more than capable of taking a few bullets," replied Donovan.

"What about silver bullets dowsed in holy water?" asked Andre.

"I'd never tell anyone what my true weakness is," responded Donovan. Andre and Donovan crawled down low near the gate. They rolled and crawled until they eventually approached the mansion. Donovan broke the lock on a window and they quickly jumped inside— only to realize they had stumbled right into a room of about six revenants, who all pointed their guns at them.

Arnold emerged from the shadows and said, "Ah, how nice of you to join us. You're just in time for the fun."

Chapter 41

The next morning, Hunter drove to the usual location and a homeless man immediately started walking beside him. "They're coming, you know," said the homeless man. His teeth were rotted and his breath smelled even worse. He had a grey, patchy beard, filthy, tattered clothes, and bloodshot eyes. Hunter eased away from the man until the man grasped him by the arm. "The Forgotten Ones will rise, hehehehe," said the man, it was now apparent that he was ill. He violently coughed, his face was covered in red blotches, and he was struggling to breathe.

"Let go of me, ya wanker! Bloody hell, you're a damned bio-hazard. Stay the hell away from me before you get me sick, too," yelled Hunter. The man was dribbling blood from his mouth and then gave him a smile. Hunter walked away. The homeless man did not follow.

He went into the hideout. The Boss was in the usual chair, the mysterious leather-bound book from yesterday on his desk. "Morning Boss," said Hunter.

"Morning. Turns out that your lil' fuck-up yesterday is bearing some fruit. I did a bit of research on this book here and it's part of a collection of ancient human leather-bound mystic books called the *Canticum*—this one being *Canticum Robiginem* which translates to 'Blight Song' in Latin. Now obviously, I don't believe in witchcraft and the like, but there is profit to be made. I have a buyer lined up who is willing to buy it for an amount which will cover the cost of your slipup and then some. So, I'm giving you one more chance. You fuck this up . . . and it's your head. You, your little wife, and your boy's heads. Are we clear?" said the Boss.

"Don't you dare rope them into my mess! I swear if you hurt them I'll—" said Hunter.

"You'll what?" responded the Boss as Boris and Armando showed up. Hunter angrily grumbled and took the book. He stormed out of the hideout.

Hunter slid the book into his coat pocket and walked to his car, he began to hear a voice whisper to him, "Open the book." Nightingale quickly turned around and there was no one there. The whisper repeated—this time sharper and caused a pressure in his head. "Open the book and all shall be revealed. You will find the Truth of this world," said the voice.

He quickly headed to his car. "Well, I suppose one little look wouldn't hurt," said Hunter, "Ancient mystical book? Yeah, right.

Old cauldron witch rubbish." He pulled the book out and felt the cover—a chill ran down his spine as he touched the ancient human leather. He opened the book and there were several sketches and handwritten paragraphs of a language he did not recognize. The black ink began to glow red in response to his touch. "What the hell?" he said.

A rush of power swept over him and he was now floating around in the Void. He came face to face with a mass of boil-covered tendrils. Beneath the mass of tendrils was an obsidian skinned man with red markings all over his body. He was completely nude, but there were not any genitalia to be seen. He had glowing red eyes. His fingers were gangrenous: a mix of green, yellow, and black. The only hair that was on his body was a beard of red, an almost scarlet color. His body was bony and thin, as though he had been starved for an eternity, yet he seemed fine. He sat atop a throne, and Nightingale called out to him. "W-Where the hell am I?" demanded Hunter.

"Do not fear, Hunter Nightingale Sr. It is a pleasure to meet you. I am Scar-li-homun, the Motivator of Sickness and Blight," replied the ancient being.

"I-I don't understand. Where am I?" responded Nightingale.

"Is it not obvious? The *Canticum* has brought you here. This is the Void, the Realm of the Forgotten Ones," said Scar-li-homun.

"How do I get back?! I want to go back! Look, you can keep your Canti-whatever; I just want out of here!" said Hunter.

"Oh? Do you wish to put your family in danger? Why fear that pathetic whelp you call 'Boss'? Why throw away an opportunity to gain power and destroy all who oppose you?" said the ancient being.

"By making a deal with a Devil?" asked Nightingale.

"Fool! I am no Devil. I am a Forbidden One, one of The Existence's abandoned children. The Void strengthened us; it gave us power beyond your simple human understanding. I know what it is that you desire: you seek to improve your station; allow me to help you. Become a Bearer of my power, abandon all you know of the World, and I shall open your eyes to the Truth," said Scar-li-homun.

"I don't know . . . this is so much to take in, I'm literally floating an empty Void of nothing and talking an ancient being beyond my understanding," said Hunter.

"Perhaps you simply need time to think on it . . . keep the book for now," said Scar-li-homun.

"But I have to sell it . . . to protect my family," said Nightingale.

"You let me worry about that, human. One can never truly possess a *Canticum*," said the eldritch entity. And with a bright flash, Hunter was brought back to his reality. The book was tossed away from him. *Fucking Hell . . . can anything ever go my way?* thought Hunter.

"They shall, Hunter Nightingale Sr. Now drive to the pickup place," said Scar-li-homun.

"Good Lord! Now you're in my head!" said Nightingale.

"Do not say that old Fool's name! It infuriates me . . . now drive!" said Scar-li-homun.

Nightingale did as instructed and arrived at the docks, where the buyer was waiting to buy the book. Hunter deeply breathed and grabbed the book. He put it in a paper bag and got out to meet the buyer, who had two other people with him, "Ah, you must be the supplier. I understand you are in possession of a *Canticum*. I have your money ready. I hope you don't mind that I bought two assistants just in case things go south," said the man.

"Ah, a foolish priest, thinking that he can destroy my *Canticum* with a few incantations and blessings," said Scar-li-homun.

"I sense a presence besides ours . . . " said one of the guards behind the buyer.

"And an exorcist? How amusing," chuckled the eldritch being.

"It is possible that there are supernatural beings nearby. I specially gave word to the supplier's Boss not to let anyone read it. Not even himself," said the buyer.

"Uh, right of course. Very clear instructions not to do so. Anyways, you have the money?" asked Nightingale.

A man pulls out the case of money and Hunter thoroughly made sure all the money was in there.

"Is your inspection done? My associates and I have other things we must do today," said the buyer with an outstretched palm.

"Of course," said Hunter as he passed the brown bag to him. The buyer said, "Well, that was simple."

"Yeah . . . it was," said Hunter as he felt a force take over. He released a horde of rats over the buyer and his guards.

The rats squeaked and shrieked as they attacked the guards. The associates took out guns but could not draw them fast enough as the rats began to rip and tear into them. Hunter looked at his own hands to see the mess he caused. His eyes were glowing red. The rats continued to attack the buyer and his associates until they become infected with a disease Hunter could not even put a name to. They began to fervently beg for the Lord to protect them as they violently coughed blood and profusely bled from orifices. Their limbs began to necrotize very rapidly; their skin became very withered and blackened. They couldn't do anything but scream as they rotted away to nothing, Hunter ran away as the rats began to devour them down to nothing. Roaches and flies collected what was left of the three, erasing all evidence of their existence. Hunter got into his car, hyperventilating and eyes widened as looked at the passenger seat: the book and the money were there.

"See? I told you I would take care of things. Now . . . let's head back to that Boss of yours," said Scar-li-homun.

"I . . . I took human life. Three of them. I've never done that before," said Hunter.

"And how did that make you feel?" asked the being. Hunter smiled for moment. He then replied, "Powerful . . . but . . . I don't know if—"

"You will never get what you want if you bring weak thoughts into your mind like morals. Now come now, let's go to your Boss," said Scar-li-homun.

Hunter went into the hideout. He had the book in his pocket and the case of money in his hand. The Boss now had a skull on his desk and said to him, "Oh? Back so soon? Got my money?"

Hunter laid it on the table and the Boss personally counted it himself. "Good! Good! It's all here. Wonderful, all right then . . . Boris, kill him. Armando, get the door if you please." Armando locked the door and Boris pulled out a gun,

"The fuck is this? I did as I was told!" said Hunter.

"I know. But people like you are hazardous to business—I cannot tolerate mistakes," said the Boss. Boris unloaded shots directly at Hunter's center of mass, causing him to collapse.

"Such a treacherous fool. Now will you accept my power?" said Scar-li-homun as Hunter was bleeding out on the floor.

Chapter 42

Arnold pointed the barrel of a rifle at Andre and Donovan, looking down the sights, safety off.

"Kid, I know this isn't you. It's Nightingale's magic taking control of your ghost; please come back to your senses. All of you," said Andre as he tried to emit his influence amongst the revenants. He did so by trying to exert dominion over their ghosts using his power. They began to hold their heads in pain with one hand, but their eyes went devoid once more and they were brought back under control.

"Lun's tricks will not work upon these poor souls, Moonchild. They are under my subjugation," said Arnold with the obvious demeanor of Nightingale. He walked around while the other revenants kept their guns on the duo. Arnold closed the window and said, "It was not my intent to arouse all of the suspicion of others. I only wanted to pick off the junkies and bums at first. Society's undesirables. But my Lord demanded more suitable candidates for the revenant transformation."

"Why would you want to summon a Forbidden One into this world? The Motivator of Disease, no less?" asked Andre.

"Simple. I owe him my life. After my father killed my mother by misusing the dark Lord's power, he took his own life. The *Canticum* called out to me . . . and it saved me. He saved me from a cruel world that does not care for plights and sorrows of the downtrodden. After the media receives their repugnant attention-seeker stories . . . no one cares about what happens to the kid afterwards. I was beaten, abused, broken in more ways than I could count. But one day, Lord Scar-li-homun's book called out to me. And when it did—it gave me the same power that had consumed my father, but unlike him, I was smarter with it. I escaped my circumstances, climbed my way with the rapidity of a mad man, and gained all that I wanted within this world. And all I had to do was spread The Diseased King's works throughout the world. Ever wondered why there are so many disease-afflicted villages and outbreaks? That is the work of me and my network, because much more gets done as a team. And as a team, called the Fester, we have served our Lord diligently since this point. And I intend to do his will and bring him into this world so that he may share his gifts and usher us along with his siblings into the new era. Try as you might to fight but you will fail. And you will be added to the pile of corpses that I have laid to gain my kingdom," said Nightingale-Arnold.

Arnold snapped back to "normal" and he said, "What just happened?"

The other revenants kept their guns pointed at Donovan and Andre. After regaining his bearings, Arnold said, "Time to die." He raised up his hand, eager to give the word for the revenants to fire.

Donovan asked, "Is it time to die?" Arnold scoffed and turned around. A large horse appeared, seemingly out of nowhere! It charged at him with full force and the impact of its body against Arnold knocked him down to the ground. It was a mare that was black as coal, its eyes were a blazing red. It had a flowing mane of pure white and on its head were two horns. She then gave a mighty neigh and the other revenants were confused as to where this mysterious mare came from! They did not know what to do, other than to fire their guns. She impaled another revenant on her horns and effortlessly flicked him off them. She knocked over another revenant and trampled on her. She easily stomped on the revenant's head as if it were a pumpkin. In the confusion, Andre pulled out his gun and capped one of the revenants in the face. He then hit it in the face with a clay matrix using his Yonica. The impact was so hard that the clay matrix exploded! The shrapnel afflicted several other revenants, turning them to dust. Arnold narrowly escaped and the rest of the revenants were easily dispatched. The mare approached Donovan. She puffed up a gust of smoke and patiently looked at him. Donovan rubbed her snout and said, "Good girl. Thank you, Shadow."

"Shadow? Who's this horse?" asked Andre.

"She's my horse. Shadow II. Shadow I was a real stubborn mare, but her daughter took to me as well as she did," responded Donovan.

"Still doesn't explain how she got in here," said Andre.

Donovan replied, "It's a long story, I'll explain later. Arnold is probably running his precious master right now. We gotta be ready to fight. All right Shadow, get on, girl. Go on, git." Shadow puffed out another bit of smoke and disappeared in a blaze of blackened hellfire.

Andre snatched a stray ghost from one of the mounts of dust and said, "I need to borrow your memories for a second."

"I don't understand what is going on, but you saved me. Please do what you can to save the other people," responded the ghost. He touched them and their memories revealed many things to him. Through the hazy vision of the revenant, Ginny was dangling over the inner foyer. Underneath it was a massive circle swirling with evil energies. Andre caught a glimpse of the Void. Inside it was the withered form of Scar-li-homun sitting there, simply waiting. The ancient being devoured the power of spirits and pumped blood into himself. The Forbidden One looked upon him and said nothing. It merely shot him a soul-piercing stare. In that moment, Andre began to feel very itchy. He started to scratch himself, but the itch could not be satisfied. His body began to dissolve into pieces! He was slowly melting due to some sort of unknown disease! Andre began to shout in sheer horror!

Donovan shook him back to his senses. He yelled, "Kid, are you all right? Andre!"

Andre snapped back to his senses and took a moment to regain his composure. He replied, "I'm fine. I'm fine. It looks like we won't be able to get the leg up on this one with the ghosts' help this time." Andre turned to the ghost and said, "Thank you anyway. Please have a wonderful rest. I promise I will save as many of you as I can." The ghost nodded and then smiled. They faded away to the afterlife.

Donovan said, "This is why humans invented maps." He pulled out the plans of the mansion. He looked at it and pointed to an area, "We are in one of the living rooms; by my guess, if we go through this door going forward it should bring us to the main hall." Donovan summoned his sword in blaze of black hellfire.

Andre rolled up his sleeve and then flexed his Yonica. In his other hand, he held his staff. "So, we are on the first floor and we have to make it to the third floor before it is too late. Hopefully, Arnold hasn't gotten back to his master yet. He's likely going to try to impede advancement to the inner foyer," said Andre. He used the Yonica to create a small projection of the map for himself. Andre and Donovan walked out to the hall and there were several cloaked figures. They were likely magi of the Fester, ready to defend the summoning of their Master at any cost.

Chapter 43

"Yes . . . " said Hunter very weakly. His eyes began to glow and he steadily rose up from the ground.

"What the fuck!" yelled Armando. He raised his gun and shot at Hunter once more, but the bullets barely make him stagger. Hunter grabbed Armando by the throat. Armando screamed as his organs ripped out of his body. Armando's unharmed organs assimilated into Hunter's body, healing the bullet wounds. Boris quickly tried to reload his gun, but Hunter threw Armando's lifeless body at Boris's legs. His legs shattered upon impact, ripping into the femoral arteries. Boris bled profusely and he tried to maintain a breath, albeit a very raggedy one. Flies broke through the window and surrounded Boris and Armando. They bit them, infecting them both with the same disease as before. Quick necrosis began to set in, just as before. The Boss was huddled in the corner, shaking in fear. He watched as his two lackeys melted to nothing. "W-What do you want? You want this money? You can have it. That launderer position? It's yours. Hell, you can even have my job! Just please, for The Existence's sake, man, spare my life!" pleaded the Boss.

"You know, Cornelius . . . I've always hated your mug. So arrogant, greedy, and cowardly," said Hunter. "And honestly, I'm not going to touch you. You're that pathetic in my eyes. You aren't worth bloodying my hands over . . . but a rat?" said Hunter. A ravenous rat hissed and snarled at the Boss. "I think you and he are more alike than you think. As a matter of fact, why don't you both get more acquainted?" said Hunter. He commanded the rat to burrow right into Cornelius's eye. The rat leaped onto Cornelius, who closed his eyes shut. The rat clawed its way past his eye lid and then forced itself through his eyeball. A visceral squelching sound could be heard as the eyeball was squished. While this is going on, Cornelius was screaming in pure pain and fear. He tried to grab the tail of the rat, but to no avail. He flailed about. He banged his head against the wall and fell to the ground. "Don't eat his brain yet, little guy. I want him to be conscious enough to suffer for as long as possible before the disease gets to him. You all can feast on the rest of him though," said Hunter. More rats crawled into the window and began to feast upon Cornelius. Hunter buttoned up his coat to hide his blood-covered shirt. Hunter got out of the building and walked away. Cornelius's screams continued to be heard as he was ripped apart by the rats. Eventually, he could not even fight back. The disease was in him. His limbs rotted off and he melted to nothingness.

Hunter drove home, a malicious smile on his face. "That was such a rush! What's next?" he asked.

"Now, now, my little acolyte, this next part is very exciting. That occurs tomorrow. Head home for now," said Scar-li-homun. Hunter parked the car in his driveway. His wife Rebecca had her things loaded up in her car. She had little Hunter Jr. holding her hand. Hunter slammed the door; his red eyes were now brown once more. He walked up to her and asked, "The hell's all this then?"

"I can't take this anymore. I can't stand this life and I don't want the poisonous life you are so hell-bent on living infecting our son any longer. I'm leaving you!" yelled Rebecca.

"Love, come on now. You don't mean that; look I gained power—"

"Power this! Power that! You seem to love power much more than you love me. Well, tell you what, you and your whore Power can do whatever the hell you bloody feel like. Because I am done. And so is our son Hunter Jr." said Rebecca. She tried to walk away from him with Hunter Jr. still holding her hand. But Hunter Sr. grabbed her by the arm. She let go of Hunter Jr.

"You aren't leaving me. Neither is our son," said Hunter Sr, with a grave tone in his voice.

"Let go of me or I'll call the bloody cops. Just who do you think you are?" yelled Rebecca. She tried to wriggle out of Hunter Sr.'s iron-tight grip. She noticed the blood on him and she screamed, "Hunter Jr! Run to the neighbors, tell them to call the poli—"

Hunter Sr. grasped his wife by the mouth and her mouth was filled with roaches. The roaches crawled down her mouth and started to fill up her internal organs but she could not scream due to the roaches blocking her airway. She was now infected. She fell to her knees. She coughed and gagged and tried to spit up the roaches. But there were too many. As she suffocated, Hunter Sr. began to regain control of his senses. He feebly tried to get the roaches out of her mouth, but it was too late. She was dead. Tears welled up his eyes. "Oh my word . . . what have you made me do?" yelled Hunter Sr. Hunter Jr. was in shock and he didn't say anything.

"I am removing the thing that makes you weak. Now you kill your son as well. Or do you wish to relinquish my power?" said Scar-li-homun.

"If this is what it takes to gain power . . . THEN TO HELL WITH IT!" yelled Hunter Sr.

"Pathetic fool—very well then," said Scar-li-homun. The roaches crawled out of Rebecca and began to crawl over Hunter Sr. The roaches began to tear into his flesh, and in his struggle, he knocked out the book. It landed toward Hunter Jr. "No, no, no! Son, don't open that book for the love of all that is holy! Run!" yelled Hunter. He tried to run over to his son, but he fell to the ground. His limbs began to necrotize.

"Perhaps your son will do a better job of serving me than you did. Children are so much easier to teach the ways of the Truth," said Scar-li-homun. The last thing that Hunter Sr. saw was his son opening the *Canticum*. The words glowed red as they had before for him.

Eventually, the police investigated the mysterious disappearances of what later became known as the Scar-li-homun Murders. Mr. and Mrs. Nightingale's corpses were found in front of their homes. Their bodies were surrounded by an infestation of vermin. They had dispersed the second the police approached the bodies. When an autopsy had been done, it showed that the couple had died of anthrax first. But they could never find the exact origin of what caused Mr. Nightingale's limbs to melt off. They were survived by their young son, Hunter Nightingale Jr. He was found sobbing over the loss of his parents. After a period of being quarantined, he was placed into foster care. Eventually all trace of him disappeared from the U.K.

Chapter 44

Arnold could be seen hobbling along the stairs. One of his legs was slightly damaged from a matrix explosion. He ran up the stairs to the second floor. The Fester magi drew out their staffs. The three of them cast a lightning spell that combined into one large bolt. Andre put up a defensive shield to cover them. Donovan willed hellfire to his command and threw several fireballs at the magi. "The Fester will not be beaten, fools!" yelled Harold. He began to twitch and convulse. His hood fell off and his eyes rolled into the back of his head. His eyes popped out and bone began to protrude out His entire skull and his spine ripped out of his head. The remnant fleshy, bony mass formed some sort of horrific bat-like creature. It screeched a human-like scream and vomited boiling blood towards the duo. Andre and Donovan rolled out of the way and the blood slowly seeped into the ground.

"What the fuck is that?!" yelled Donovan.

"I don't know, some sort of brain bat thing?!" responded Andre. Andre ran behind a pillar and chucked a flame spear at one of the other magi. When the spear hit him, he burst into flames. His flesh screamed after he collapsed.

The Brain Bat Harold flapped in the air and said in a raspy voice, "Fool! We are The Fester! No matter how many you kill, we shall continue to spread!" The other magi took on hideous forms. Their bones violently erupted out and their flesh molded a new shape. There was a gorilla-like creature. Its fists were enlarged and covered in rows of sharp bone. The creature's face was a normal human skull with several eyeballs on it. The other magi had become an elongated mass of flesh and bone. It was similar in shape to a serpent. Only one enlarged veiny eye appeared on it. The interior of its mouth was covered in rows of teeth like a shark or a lamprey. The last magi became some sort of odd mix of humanoid and centaur. The anatomy of their bones made no logical sense, the tatters of their black robe remained. From their forearm, the centaur pulled out a chunk of bone. The chunk of bone became elongated and sharp.

"That was the most disgusting thing I've ever seen in my life," said Andre.

"Eh, I've seen worse," said Donovan. Donovan threw some hellfire as a distraction and the duo ran up the stairs in opposing directions. The serpent and centaur went after Donovan. The brain bat and gorilla went after Andre.

Brain Bat Harold flapped over Andre and started to project vomit and more boiling, bloody bile at Andre. He screamed when a bit of it got on him. It had slightly burned his back, but thankfully did not leak through. The serpent slithered toward

Donovan with such an insane amount of speed. He pulled out his gun and shot it in the eye. The creature was barely phased by this. The centaur quickly advanced on Donovan. It slashed at him with its bone blade. Donovan narrowly blocked it and cut the blade in half with his own sword. The bone regenerated as quickly as he sliced it off. The gorilla began to huff and puff as it chased Andre. It grabbed him by the Yonica. Andre experienced some whiplash from being suddenly forced to stop and fell flat on the ground. The gorilla tried to stomp on Andre, but Andre disconnected the prosthetic and rolled out of the way. Harold flew over Andre and tried to vomit more blood onto him. Andre stuck his staff in his mouth and shouted, "Freeze!" The ice erupted from the top of the staff. The ice pierced right through Harold's mutated face. The blood immediately chilled and Andre smacked the gorilla with the frozen brain bat. Harold's icy visage shattered to pieces upon impact.

Andre valiantly tapped his staff into the ground, ready to take the gorilla down with only one arm. He tossed his staff up into the air as a distraction, and the gorilla stampeded through what was left of Harold. Andre cast lighting from his hand to distract the beast. He jumped up and smashed it over the head with his staff. A loud crack could be heard from the impact of the staff against the gorilla's skull. Andre snatched the Yonica back and quickly reattached it. He stabbed the gorilla with several spears of blazing blue flame. Andre snapped his fingers and the spears exploded. The beast fell to the ground. Its flesh tried to twist and contort to another form, but the damage was too severe. It melted into a charred liquid. Andre turned around to the action happening near him. Donovan was fending off the centaur to the best of his ability, but he quickly got wrapped up by the serpent.

Donovan groaned as was he squeezed by the powerful grip of the serpent. The centaur walked slowly towards Donovan with a bone blade in hand. Donovan let out a mighty breath of fire as if he were a dragon. His eyes began to glow purple and horns erupted from his head. With significant strain, he broke free from the grip of the snake. He then grabbed it as if it were a lasso and swung it around. He gave a mighty yell as he chucked the serpent at the centaur. The serpent knocked back the centaur. He summoned his blade and sliced up the serpent into tiny cubes. The cubes violently shook and began to twist and contort. Donovan raised up his hands and set the cubes afire. The cubes were burned to a charred liquid. Donovan willed chains from Hell that wrapped around the dazed centaur. He rammed his sword right into the chest of the creature. With a single swing upward, he bisected the massive creature. Donovan turned his back to the bisected centaur. Its flesh tried to transform once more. With his back turned, he held out the palm of his hand and fired a massive fireball at the remains. The fireball pushed the body all the way back to the end of the hall. The corpse was burned to cinders. There was nothing left, and the chains of Hell sucked back into the ground. Donovan's features went back to his usual self and he noticed Andre. Andre was in disbelief at Donovan's display of power. Donovan snapped him out of it when he said, "What? This ain't my first scuffle. Let's go to the third floor. I hope we're not too late."

Chapter 45

Arnold hobbled toward the other revenants. He tripped and then quickly picked himself back up. He slammed the massive door of the inner foyer and Cindy re-cast the seal over it. She yelled, "What the hell are you doing? Do you have any idea how much power it takes to keep that area sealed?"

"They're coming!" responded Arnold. He quickly picked himself up once more. His body was steadily crumbling to dust. Cindy scoffed and cast a spell to repair the damage done to his body. "Then let them. They won't be able to stop us in time to save their little friend from the sacrifice spell. I'll radio the boss," said Cindy. She pulled out a walkie talkie and said, "Master Nightingale, the intruders have almost arrived. We need to per-form that spell now!"

Nightingale replied, "I still need more time before the spell is cast, one miscalculation and all this effort and ghosts will be for nothing! Now distract them!"

Cindy looked at Arnold and then said "But I—"

"But what? Did I make a mistake in making you my protégé?" asked Nightingale.

"No. You didn't. Your will shall be done, Master" said Cindy. "Good. Then get it done," said Nightingale. She sighed and Arnold put an empathetic hand on her shoulder. She smacked it away and pulled him by the arm. "C'mon. I'm going to make you even stronger," said Cindy. She stole energy from several other revenants, who screamed but could do nothing. The energy flowed directly into Arnold. This process turned those revenants to dust. Arnold and Cindy walked out of the room.

A few moments later, Andre and Donovan punched through the first barrier of the third floor with little effort. "That wasn't too hard to break. It was probably cast by some sort of novice," said Andre.

"NOVICE?! I'LL SHOW YOU, YOU IGNORANT FOOL!" yelled Cindy with obvious fury in her voice.

"Ah yes, I'm definitely afraid. Novice," said Andre with hateful intent in his tone. Andre smacked his staff into the ground and easily dispelled the ward covering the door. Suddenly, several revenants burst the door wide open! Arnold was amongst them. He was fully repaired, but his eyes were now completely white. He emanated some sort of new power. "How's it going, fellas? Missed me?" he asked. In his hand, he held a polearm.

"You handle the jobbers, I'll handle Archie Comics over here," said Andre. Andre flexed his Yonica; blue energy emanated from the arm. Arnold pointed the polearm at Andre. "I'd like to see what you can do, Moonchild," he said. Donovan nodded and

took flight. He flew overhead and slashed apart several revenants. Andre and Arnold fought each other.

Andre said, "This can only end one way, man. I know this
isn't you. It's the magic of that bitch over there. Who is Nightingale's bitch, pretty much making you the bitch of a bitch. Give it
up and take this matrix."

"I'd like to see you try. And I'll thank you not to insult my
girlfriend," responded Arnold. He dreamily looked at her and
blew her a kiss. Cindy swooned a little and Andre sighed. He
chucked a clay matrix at him. The clay matrix simply shattered,
and nothing happened to Arnold.

"What the hell did she do to you?" said Andre with a look of
shock.

"You won't figure it out in time. I wonder what a revenant
Moonchild is like?" responded Arnold. He flexed and twirled
around the polearm. He stabbed and slashed at Andre with it!
Andre parried the blows and rolled out of the way of a few of
his strikes.

Donovan cleared out the field, bisecting revenants and
punching the heads off others. One managed to get a good
lick on him. Donovan flinched a little, but then responded by
grabbing the one who grabbed him. He smashed the revenant's
head in with a clay matrix. It evaporated to dust. Donovan split
the matrix in half and used it like dual daggers. Once halves
were inside the revenants, he would combine them together.
Donovan yelled to Andre, "If you need help, I don't mind helping

you1 These revenants ain't going anywhere!" Donovan punched another revenant in the face.

Andre responded, "I got it!" Andre narrowly dodged Arnold's polearm.

Arnold yelled, "DIE!"

Andre threw a flaming javelin and it exploded inside Arnold! The small explosion barely made him flinch. Cindy laughed and said, "You should just give up! You can't possibly defeat my precious Arnold!" Andre parried Arnold's next volley attacks. With a free opening, Andre used his Yonica to hit him with a supercharged sprit punch.

Arnold merely flinched and mockingly asked, "Was that supposed to hurt?"

"Nah, just had to find out what was up with you. She turned you into a lich. You don't have a ghost in there anymore. Your ghost is basically attached via a wireless connection. A phylactery. I bet Blondie over there has it on her," said Andre. His attention turned over to Cindy, who tried to run off, but Donovan was blocking the way. He had his sword and shook dust off it. Cindy grumbled and a fleshy growth spawned from one of her arms. It was a whip-like structure. She used it to stab into Donovan and chucked him out of the way. Donovan pulled out his gun and shot her in the amulet, causing Arnold's ghost to come out. He screamed in pain and then heavily panted. Arnold's main body finally crumbled to dust. Cindy ran up to the final door. She used her mutated arm to erect a fleshy barrier to the entrance of the inner foyer.

Donovan collapsed to the ground and said, "Don't worry, kid. I'm all right." He quickly kickflipped up and Andre went over to the ghost of Arnold.

Arnold's ghost said, "Thank you. Thank you so much. I don't know how I can thank you enough . . . the things I've done, the things I've seen. I was just dating that . . . that demoness and she killed me. And put me in that hellish scape. I am so sorry."

"It's fine. You're fine. Just do me a favor and have a good rest. We'll save the others like you," said Andre. He helped Arnold's ghost pass on. The duo heard Ginny scream and Andre yelled out, "Ginny!" They ran up to the barrier and Andre threw several spears of fire at the barrier. They exploded and easily incinerated the barrier. Cindy ripped her tentacle arm out of the ground and Nightingale slit Ginny's throat.

Chapter 46

"GINNNYYYYY!" yelled Andre as Nightingale dropped her to the ground. Her blood completed the summons and her spirit began to leave her body. "I REFUSE TO LET YOU DIE HERE!" yelled Andre as his eyes glowed blue. He cast his hand out and forcefully tethered Ginny's spirit back into its body.

Cindy yelled, "Impossible!"

Andre grabbed Ginny and gave her to Donovan. He said to him, "Get her help now. I don't know how long I can force her spirit back into her body."

"I-I knew you'd save me . . . " croaked out Ginny. She held her neck to keep more blood from gushing out.

Andre took off his cloak and used it to apply pressure. Donovan continued to apply pressure on her wound. He nodded to Andre and jumped from a third-floor window. He landed with ease and sprinted with inhuman speed out onto the street. He commandeered a vehicle and drove as fast as he could. "NOW

IT'S JUST YOU AND ME, NIGHTINGALE!" yelled Andre. Andre's voice was booming, making the mansion quake.

Nightingale quickly grabbed Cindy and she yelled, "Master! What are you do—UGH!"

He slit her throat and her spirit was quickly absorbed by the portal. He dropped her corpse and said to her, "I'm sorry, my dear. I truly am. But NOTHING will stop me from summoning our lord into this world. Not even you. Scar-li-homun, thanks you for your sacrifice."

"Bastard!" yelled Andre.

Massive tentacles erupted from the portal and slowly raised up Scar-li-homun's main body. Nightingale laughed, "Fool! You have lost! You cannot defeat my lord! No matter how you may try! You shall fail!" His eye began to glow a deathly red and his body began to mutate. He melted into a dark toxic sludge and reformed into a much more powerful muscular form. Andre threw several flame javelins at the tentacles. The explosions made them let out a powerful scream and they slinked back into the Void. Nightingale jumped down from the stairs and easily swatted Andre out of the way. Tentacles moved around where his mouth once was and said, "Foolish Moonchild! FKJS-FJSFHSFH." The rest of what he said was incomprehensible as human speak.

Andre felt a sizzling effect on his arm from the smack Nightingale gave him. Nightingale ran up and easily grabbed him by the neck. Andre felt a burning sensation on his neck. The tentacles from the portal rose up once more and there was nothing that could be done. Andre fell unconscious and he awoke in a realm of blue. He was in Lun's chambers! He saw the figure of the Primordial Titan.

"My descendant. You cannot be defeated here. It is not your time. I bestow upon you another portion of my power for the moment. Obliterate Scar-li-homun and all of his ilk," echoed the powerful voice of Lun. Andre nodded and he awakened in the real world. He broke out of the clutches of Nightingale! His entire body was blue now! The Yonica fell off and another glowing arm grew in its place. The night sky was out and the moon was full. He raised his hand and said, "Begone, abomination," in the voice of Lun. He blasted the body of Nightingale into a puddle with a beam from his hand. The puddle took its time to reform. The presence of Scar-li-homun's head in the world turned the sky purple. The moon struggled to stay centered. The upper body of the being was out of the portal and said, "Foolish Lun. You cannot defeat me or your older siblings. Prepare to di—"

Before he could finish, Andre-Lun flew up and punched Scar-li-homun in the face. The being's face began to shake and then shattered into more tentacles. Andre-Lun easily ripped off the tentacles of the being. He then blasted several beams of blue energy at Scar-li-homun's massive body. The being's upper body was badly burned. "You may elude the wrath of Father, but you shall not escape mine," said Andre-Lun as they flew in front of the massive being. He blasted the powerful being into bits and pieces. Scar-li-homun summoned pests from all over the city to his side, but it was to no avail. Andre-Lun slaughtered the beasts and collected their spirits. The ghosts of the slain pests were turned against the Forbidden One.

Scar-li-homun yelled, "You may win this day, but this is not the last you will hear of me!" The Forbidden One tried to slink back into the portal, but Andre-Lun grabbed it by the arm.

He said, "There is no next time for you." He ripped Scar-li-homun's arm apart and then summoned a blade made of pure energy. Andre-Lun slashed apart Scar-li-homun's massive body, breaking it into tiny pieces before blasting the pieces into dust. The summoning portal closed and the bottom half of Scar-li-homun fell deep into the Void. Andre-Lun gently landed to the ground. Andre felt the presence of Lun leave him and he lost the projection arm. He collapsed to the ground. Andre screamed in pain as phantom pain set in, his stump violently shaking. Andre struggled to get back up.

Due to the fight, the mansion was crumbling! After Andre steadied his breathing, he crawled over to his Yonica. The wraith of Nightingale came out of the woodworks and yelled, "BASTAR-RRD! YOU RUINED EVERYTHING THAT TOOK ME OVER TWENTY YEARS TO BUILD! MY CULT, GONE! MY MASTER, GONE! ALL OF IT! YOU SHALL PAY WITH YOUR LIFE." The wraith easily pummeled the downed Andre. Andre tried to regain control of his senses but could not. He bled from his stump and had a ragged breath. He managed to roll over to his staff and stabbed into the wraith. He cast an ice spell and the ice stabbed into the wraith. It let out a horrendous scream and then flew at Andre. Andre threw a clay matrix at the wraith. The wraith felt a sizzling pain when the matrix hit its body. Andre was fading in and out of consciousness, but he kept a clay matrix close to him. The wraith was nowhere near as coherent as the actual Nightingale. The facets of his spirit were so corrupted and spawned from hate. Andre fell to the ground and finally lost consciousness.

"It appears that you are having some issues, Andre," echoed the voice of Nahid.

They were transported to a dark void. Nahid's true form could be seen: he appeared as an Arabian man with a short beard, a long ponytail, and several earrings. He wore a purple outfit. "So what say I take care of this wraith problem for you? It will cost you only one wish," said Nahid.

"Fuck that. Even if you do that, the mansion will still fall on me. I know how you djinns like to play with loopholes. Besides, that'll break one of the seals on my car," responded Andre, still on the ground.

"Ah yes, then die and leave the city only to Donovan and Ginny. They certainly could find another Moonchild to take your place. It's not like your kind are rare or anything like that. Tell you what . . . I'll make this one wish a two-parter. I'll take care of your wraith problem AND I'll take you to the hospital. All you have to do is say yes. Look, I don't like you. And you don't like me. But it's very apparent that you're important to keeping a healthy spirit ecosystem around here. So let me help you this once. I think Ginny deserves that, don't you?" argued Nahid.

Andre sighed and then replied, "Fine. Fucking fine. One wish it is. No bullshit though." Nahid smiled and said, "Very well." He snapped his fingers and the car revved to life. It flew to the mansion! Andre awakened with the wraith mere inches away from him. Nahid's spirit came out and easily obliterated the spirit. Nahid cauterized Andre's wound with his wave of his hand and levitated him into the car. "That should hold that wound until we get you actual help," said Nahid. Nahid drove Andre quickly to the hospital and ejected him out of the passenger seat, in front of the ER. Nahid drove away into a random parking lot. Two very confused EMTS came out and wheeled Andre into the ER. One of them put an oxygen mask on him and Andre passed out once more.

Chapter 47

Andre woke up. He was hooked up to an IV on his only arm. He turned his head and there were Ginny and Donovan, looking over him. Ginny was in a wheelchair and had bandages over her neck. She smiled and weakly said, "You're finally awake. So . . . Nightingale's finished, right?"

"I knew you could do it. I had complete confidence in you, kid," said Donovan.

"Yeah…he's finished. Lun took over and I vaguely remember chopping up Scar-li-homun into tiny pieces and blasting what was left into the Void," responded Andre, "I highly doubt he's dead but it should take him a while to recover."

"Maybe even longer, since I managed to grab this," said Donovan. He held in his hand the *Canticum*.

"That should be put into Status Quo custody," said Ginny.

"Nah, you humans are always horny for power. I'll keep it. Far away from anyone's hands," said Donovan. He put the book into his coat pocket. The doctor came in and said, "Ah, you're finally awake, Mr. Leunis. How do you feel? You gave us quite a scare."

"I'm tougher than I look, Doc. But to answer your question, I feel a bit sore, but fine," said Andre.

"Good! When you came in, you had been thrown from a car right in front of the ER. Your stump was bleeding, luckily not too profusely. It appeared that you were very exhausted. Over all, your vitals are good. You should be out of here by later this evening. However, you, Ms. Kravitz, will have to stay a bit longer. Please go back to your room," said the doctor.

"Okay. Hey, we'll talk later, okay?" said Ginny. She coughed a bit and wheeled herself back to her room.

After she left, Donovan said to Andre, "That's one hell of a woman you're working with. You should be glad that she's on your side. I remember how she was trying to claw her way back into the fray after the doctors patched her up. Kicking my ass to get back there, but by the time I did, you did that Moonchild shit and it was all said and done. Then you got your ass dropped by that damned genie and . . . anyways, you know the rest. Great job, kid," said Donovan.

"Yeah . . . so anyways . . . we were supposed to talk, right?" said Andre.

"Yeah, let's talk then," said Donovan. He pulled up a seat.

"What are you exactly? And how did you know my dad?" asked Andre.

"Well . . . I'm a demon. Well, half demon anyway, but you already knew that. As for how I knew your father, I met him in the 80s. We eventually became friends and decided to work together. And you know what happened next. He passed. But before that he made me promise to watch over you all. I kept a watchful eye until one fateful car crash. I thought you all had died. Then a few days ago . . . you suddenly show up. Dressed as some sort of crusader fighting for the side your father was once against. Man, you looked ridiculous," responded Donovan.

"You're one to talk, looking like the damn Hamburglar's discount black cousin," said Andre.

They laughed for a bit. But then Donovan gave a heavy sigh. "Yeah, so where do we go from here?" he asked.

"I don't know. I don't think you're against me, but at the same time . . . I just don't know. There's a lot to take in here. I'm at a bit of a crossroads here," responded Andre.

"I understand. Well, tell you what. If you ever need my help again, I will come. No excuses, I assure you," said Donovan.

"Well, could you do me a favor? Remember that wraith of Mr. Robinson? Well he had a grandson and—"

"Say no more. I know how to get that young dumb ass off the street and put the old man at ease," said Donovan.

"Wait, how will you know it's him without any information?" asked Andre.

Donovan replied, "Kid, I've been searching down and corrupting bad eggs since before you were even a twinkle in your father's eye. I don't have to find them. They find me." He got up and shook Andre's hand and then left the hospital room.

What a cool guy, thought Andre to himself. *I wonder if I should ask Madame about him? Is his name really Donovan? What a mess.* Donovan could be seen out of the window; he revved up his motorcycle and drove off into the sunset. Donovan stopped at a red light and Israfil could be seen flying down above him. The angel smiled and gave Donovan a thumbs up. Donovan smiled back and gave him a thumbs up. The honking of a horn could be heard behind him. Donovan responded by flipping off the person behind him and drove off. Israfil shook his head and flew off into the Paradise. Donovan continued his long drive into the sunset. Andre laid back in bed and went to sleep.

Chapter 48

The following day, a young teenager talked with his friends about homework and girls. "Yeah, yeah, whatever, man. You and I both know that didn't happen. If it did, I'll eat my fucking hat right here and now," said the young man.

His friend replied, "Tommy, you better get that hat ready then. I'll get proof that me and Alyssa totally made out! I'm telling you it happened!"

Tommy scoffed and then said, "Sure, and I'm the Marquess of Queensbury. Later, man. I gotta go."

"All right, bro. See you later," said Tommy's friend.

Tommy got on the train and went to his usual corner of the street. He pulled up his hoodie and leaned up against a wall. He sent a text, "Where are you?"

"On my way," replied a text.

"Well hurry up. I gotta get back to my grandma's real soon. She'll get worried sick if I ain't back by curfew," replied Tommy. He waited and waited. Then when his back was turned, a black van showed up! A masked man grabbed him. He gagged Tommy and dragged him inside.

Tommy continued to fight back with all his might against his kidnapper, but the man had an inhuman strength. He knocked the teenager unconscious and drove off without a trace. Tommy was then awakened by a splash of cold water to the face. He came face to face with a masked man. "Rise and shine, kiddo," said the voice of the masked man.

"What do you want? Look, man. I don't want any trouble," said Tommy very nervously.

"Doesn't seem that way considering the fact you're making arrangements for drug drop-offs without even knowing who they are. Very dangerous; if I were a pedophile, your ass would be grass. Kid, do you have any idea how dangerous this life is?" asked the masked man.

"I'm doing what I have to provide for me and my grandma. Life hasn't been very forgiving on us since my gramps died," said Tommy.

"That's very sad to hear. Have you ever considered applying for a real job? A job that doesn't have the con of getting killed or thrown in jail?" asked the masked man.

Tommy said, "I—"

"Let me speak some knowledge on you kid. There are only two futures in this kind of life. Dead or in jail," said the man.

"What do you care? Why did you capture me, you weirdo?" yelled Tommy.

"I owe a favor to a friend who owes a favor to your gramps. I'm going to be nice and give you a choice," said the masked man. He pulled off his mask, revealing himself to be Donovan.

He cut off the bindings and looked at the kid, whose pants had a big wet stain in the middle. Donovan said, "Oh come on; did you really just piss yourself? Jesus, you need more help than I thought."

Tommy glanced down at the wet spot on his pants and looked away. "How old are you anyway?" asked Donovan.

"Sixteen. How did you know my grandpa?" asked Tommy.

"Don't worry about that. Worry about this. You know your grandfather would not want you out on these streets trying to be something that you aren't. You need to cut back on the rap music and smell the fucking roses. You need to quit," said Donovan.

Tommy looked down and said, "But my grandma . . . "

"Young man, look me in the eyes. Only cowards look down like some sort of shy puppy. Your grandma loves you. And I know it would break her little heart if she knew her grandson was out here trying to be a criminal," said Donovan.

Tommy looked at him and replied, "But I can't just leave . . . I've been drawn up into a gang; if I leave now, they might hurt my grandma. Or me."

"I already took care of that for you," said Donovan. He let down a nearby chain and down came the boss of the gang tied up on the chain. He was gagged, bloodied, and his eyes were tearing up. His speech was muffled by the gag in his mouth.

Donovan pulled off the gag and said, "See this boy, Tommy? He's under my protection now. You touch him or his grandma . . . and I'm slaughtering you and the rest of your bumfuck operation of misfits. Understand Tariq?" Tariq shakily replied, "Y-Yeah . . . "

Tommy said, "But money is tight . . . how will we survive?"

"I'm going to be giving you a job with some good people that I've known a long time. But for now, take this," said Donovan. He gave the kid a backpack full of cash.

"How did you get all of this? How are you going to tell me not to be a criminal, but you yourself are?" said Tommy in a spiteful tone.

"Because I'm a grown-ass man. You're still a kid and you should have the opportunity to grow up as one. I'm giving you that chance. Don't piss it away. Now, this job I'm giving you will be a decent one in a building. You're basically just pushing papers. That money should help you and Grammy out for now. I will tell you this once. And only once. Don't fuck this up. I'm doing this not only for you, but also because it's what your grandfather would have wanted," said Donovan.

Tommy began to tear up and said, "Thank you. For everything. It's just been so hard . . . why does life suck so much?" Tommy hugged Donovan and Donovan gave him a half-hug back.

He replied, "I know. It's a rough fucking gamble. Let me take you home. Also, you're telling your grandma what's been going on with you."

"What?" yelled Tommy.

"Yup. Honesty is the best policy and we're starting this off right. Now let's go," said Donovan. He let Tariq go and Tariq ran away for his life. Tommy and Donovan were then on his motorcycle. Tommy put on the spare helmet and held onto Donovan. They drove at a ridiculously fast speed to Tommy's house. Donovan's actions that day kept Tommy from going down a harsh life of crime.

Chapter 49

A few days had passed and Andre was already back to his regular self. Ginny was still in the hospital recovering. "Morning, Master! How are you feeling?" asked Frederica.

Fred chimed in and said, "Morning. Are you going to take care of that arrangement today?"

"Yup. I want to try and beat traffic to the park," said Andre. He got a call and answered it," Hello?" The familiar voice of Bill came through,

"Hey. It's Bill. I just wanted to commend you and Ginny once again for your work on the case of the Scar-li-homun Murders."

Andre got a big grin on his face and said, "Oh, no problem, Boss. Just doing our jobs."

"I thank you for that. I'm sorry I come off as an abrasive asshole most of the time, but seriously, thank you. You saved who you could in this case and prevented what could have been a cataclysmic problem for us," said Bill.

"Thank you, Boss," said Andre.

"You take care," said Bill. He hung up.

He got into the car and Nahid said, "Ah, you're feeling well enough to drive? How unfortunate for me. No matter. Let's go." Andre ignored Nahid and got onto the road. He got a call from Ginny and answered it via the Bluetooth on his car. "Hey, how are you doing, Kravitz?" asked Andre.

"Better than I was a few days ago. I still have to stay for a little while longer, but I just wanted to check up on you," said Ginny.

"I'm still doing fine. Just letting our stand-ins deal with the other snats that came along after we defeated Scar-li-homun," said Andre.

"I didn't do shit. You're the one who defeated him," replied Ginny.

"Oh, shut your humble ass up. You kept me grounded and sensible during that whole operation. Take credit for your part in this, okay?" said Andre.

Ginny responded, "Yeah, yeah. Whatever. That Donovan character been around lately?"

"Nah, I figured we should give each other some space for now. Things are still kind of new. Wounds are being re-opened and steadily repaired one at a time. I'm off to the park—gotta take care of that thing," said Andre.

"Oh yeah. It's really sweet that you're doing this. Get ready for some waterworks," said Ginny.

"Oh, I know. Anyways, I'm almost there. I'll visit you later, okay? I'll bring coffee," said Andre.

Andre parked the car and locked Nahid to the space. He turned around and said, "What happened a few days ago, thank you for saving my life."

"Thank nothing of it, Andre," replied Nahid.

"But you have to get this. It will not happen again. You will not get your way, understand?" said Andre.

"That is what you said back when I still had a three-wish seal. Keep believing you will be able to prevent disasters without me. See what happens," said Nahid.

Andre walked away and he heard a muffled voice from his coat! He pulled out the photo of Harris. Harris said, "Geez. How long were you going to keep me in there?"

"We're almost there. We need to keep a low-profile. You're literally a ghost in a photograph. More importantly, are you ready to see them?" asked Andre.

Harris replied, "Yes, I am. This will be as hard for them as it is for me."

Andre saw a woman and her two little girls sitting on a bench. She was as beautiful as Harris had described: blond hair, green eyes, freckles. Their daughters were a mix of his and Mrs. Harris's features. They looked no older than ten. "Mrs. Harris?" asked Andre.

"I'm here like the officers told me. Is it true? Is the bastard that did this . . . gone?" asked Mrs. Harris.

"He is. I took care of it. Personally. But more importantly, I have something, or rather someone I need to show you," said Andre. He handed her the photograph.

She grabbed it and said, "A picture?"

"More than just a picture, my love," said Harris tearfully. She immediately began to tear up and looked at Andre for answers. She asked, "H-How is this possible? This can't be real."

"It is, Mrs. Harris. That . . . is the spirit of your husband," said Andre. "

Christine . . . words cannot begin to describe how sorry I am that things are like this. I love you and our children with all my heart. Andre promised me that he would let me see you alone last time before he helped me pass on. He's a good man," said Harris. Christine began to mournfully tear up more and said, "Please . . . you can't go. Me and the girls need you. This has been so hard on us."

"Daddy . . . please don't go." "Daddy, we miss you," said the girls respectively. They bawled their eyes out.

"I'm sorry . . . but I don't have a say in that matter. My spirit must rest as my body must. If not . . . things will only become more dangerous for me and you all. Evil men like Nightingale will try to use me. I couldn't live myself if I ended up hurting you or anybody else," said Harris.

After a final goodbye and much crying, Andre released Harris from the picture. Andre turned to Harris's family and said, "Your husband was a good man. Without him, I don't think we would have gotten as far as we did to put an end to Nightingale's madness. You can hold onto me if you want to see him as he passes on," said Andre. Harris's ghost floated around them as they held hands in a circle. They saw a glimpse of Paradise. Harris's ghost reunited with his main spirit. He waved goodbye to his family and passed on. Mrs. Harris and the children hugged Andre. They thanked him for that final time to say goodbye to their beloved. He hugged them back and said, "If you ever need anything, please contact this number. Andre gave Mrs. Harris a card with Status Quo's number on it. He walked away and bid them goodbye once more.

"Another day in the life of a Moonchild . . . it never ends. But things like this make it worthwhile sometimes," said Andre.

Mending the Promise